BLOOD ACROSS THE DIVIDE

Judith Cranswick

© Judith Cranswick 2016
The moral right of the author has been asserted.

All rights reserved. No part of this publication may be reproduced, stored on a retrieval system, or transmitted in any form or by any means, without prior permission of the publisher.

All the characters and institutions in this publication are fictitious. Any resemblance to real persons, living or dead, is purely coincidental.

www.judithcranswick.co.uk

Novels by Judith Cranswick

The Fiona Mason Mysteries
Blood on the Bulb Fields
Blood in the Wine

Blood and Chocolate
Blood Hits the Wall
Blood Across the Divide
Blood Flows South

The Aunt Jessica Mysteries
Murder in Morocco
Undercover Geisha

Standalone Psychological Suspense
All in the Mind
Watcher in the Shadows
A Death too Far

Nonfiction
Fun Creative Writing Workshops for the New Writer

For more information, please visit
www.judithcranswick.co.uk

Prologue

Article from the Daily Chronicle – Thursday 15th June
BOMBMAKING EQUIPMENT FOUND IN HOUSE
OF KNOWN CIRA ACTIVIST
Police made a dawn raid on the home of Eamon McCollum in the early hours of yesterday morning. Although details have not yet been released, it is believed that a significant amount of bomb-making equipment, plus a large cache of arms, was discovered in an adjoining lockup.

McCollum has never made any secret of his support for a united Ireland and his opposition to what he views as the British occupation of Northern Ireland. In his youth, he was convicted twice for minor offences and, despite stories about his involvement in several atrocities that have taken in Belfast in recent years, up until now, he has always managed to avoid being brought to trial.

A local man, who refused to give his name, claimed, 'McCollum is a nasty piece of work and most people in the neighbourhood keep their heads down and go out of their way to avoid coming across his radar. It's common knowledge that he's the kingpin of the CIRA [Continuity Irish Republican Army] and it's high time he was put away. Preferably for good!'

Since the Good Friday Peace Agreement of 1998, which brought an end to the 33 years of conflict known as The Troubles, the Provisional Irish Republican Army (PIRA) and the main loyalist groups have officially ceased their terrorist campaigns and engaged with the political process. However, in recent months, the sporadic outbreaks of violence by dissident groups on both sides have escalated, and fears that a major offensive was being planned appear to be justified. One of the most active groups is the breakaway Continuity Irish Republican Army. The CIRA are opposed to the peace process and regard violence as a legitimate means of achieving their aim of a united Ireland.

Although he was never convicted, Eamon McCollum is believed to have been the mastermind behind the bomb attack outside a police station on the southern outskirts of Belfast three years ago. The attack killed three police officers and two civilians and injured several more, including two who lost limbs. The building was left in a dangerous state and had to be demolished. Several adjacent buildings also suffered substantial damage. Two men were later convicted of planting the bombs and although he was arrested and charged with planning the operation, McCollum was eventually released when insufficient evidence could be brought to procure a conviction against him after one witness was killed in a hit-and-run and two more withdrew their statements.

Beautiful Belfast and Northern Ireland

This is an exciting new tour in our Super Sun programme. Why not join us and explore all that this beautiful part of the United Kingdom has to offer? Admire the impressive buildings of its capital city together with the rugged cliff scenery of the Antrim coast; the Queen of the Glens, Glenariff, and the spectacular scenery of the Giant's Causeway.

Belfast, the fascinating historic capital of Northern Ireland, was an industrial giant in the 19th century, famed for its linen and its shipyards. The wealth these industries brought to the city is reflected in the graceful Victorian and Edwardian buildings which we will see on our tour.

The Province of Northern Ireland was created after the partition of the island in 1921. Its six counties were once part of Ulster, one of Ireland's four traditional kingdoms.

Super Sun Executive Travel
Specialists in Luxury Short Breaks and
Continental Tours

Beautiful Belfast and Northern Ireland - Passenger List

(with Fiona's added comments)

Tour Manager...Mrs Fiona Mason
Driver...Mr Winston Taylor

Mr David Cox – *Thinning grey hair, 60s, strong NE accent like his wife*
Mrs Beryl Cox – *Tiny, long dark hair, live wire despite age*
Mr Colin Davenport – *Friendly, easy-going. Black-rimmed glasses*
Mrs Louise Davenport – *Youngest in the group, ponytail, pleasant, sociable*
Mr Greg Fletcher – *Tall, dark brown hair, grey beard, birdwatcher, has a temper!*
Mrs Joan Fletcher – *50s, friendly but not one to push herself forward*
Miss Stephanie Jessen – *Pretty, mid-30s, long chestnut hair, aloof*
Mr Norman Mullins – *Medium height, unassuming, 70s*
Mrs Irene Mullins – *70s, eager to please, talkative*
Mr Chester Porter – *Late 30s, 5'10", bit intense, shy, seems pleasant*
Mr Douglas Redhill – *Pleasant enough, not pushy*

Day 1 Sunday

Our tour begins in Liverpool, famous for its architecture, its colourful maritime past, its culture and of course, as the home of the Beatles – John, Paul, George and Ringo. UNESCO declared major parts of the city a world heritage site in 2004, and in 2008, Liverpool became the European Capital of Culture.

There are many reasons to arrive early to enjoy some of the highlights of this beautiful city. Not only does it have world-class museums and art galleries, it is home to the Liverpool Philharmonic orchestra, one of the best orchestras in Europe. The city has the largest collection of Grade I listed buildings in the UK including the fine neoclassical St George's Hall and the Walker Art Gallery.

A busy port city, Liverpool is also known for its historic waterfront district and the Albert Dock, where some of the city's best-known attractions are to be found, including the Maritime Museum, the Tate Liverpool, and The Beatles Story. Close by, is the fascinating Museum of Liverpool, opened in 2012.

Our magnificent Titanic-themed hotel is a striking white and red brick building with pinnacle corner towers. It was once the offices of the world-famous White Star Shipping Line which owned the ill-fated RMS Titanic. Many features of the hotel have been retained from its early days, including a mosaic map of South America which covers the floor of the entrance hall. Each room is designed to recreate the experience of first-class passengers aboard what was once the world's premier cruise line.

The formal part of our tour begins with a small cocktail party where you will meet your fellow guests and this will be followed by an introductory briefing meeting with your experienced Tour Manager who will be with you throughout this wonderful trip to ensure that you have a perfect holiday.

Super Sun Executive Travel

One

Fiona suppressed a yawn and glanced at her watch. The hotel developers had gone to great efforts to preserve as much of the original building as possible, but after almost three hours tucked into a dark corner staring at the walls lined with black wood shelves full of old ledgers and bits and pieces from its White Star days, the charm of the place was beginning to wear a little thin.

Only one more couple to check in, but if they didn't arrive soon, she would have to leave it until the party. The so-called cocktail party – a grand title for what would be a few drinks and nibbles before dinner – was due to start in three-quarters of an hour. Apart from packing up here, she would need to check the arrangements with the hotel staff and get changed. Although it was billed as an informal affair, Fiona had no intention of turning up in the Super Sun uniform of navy-blue suit and bright yellow scarf she was currently wearing.

Perhaps she should check at the reception desk and see if the missing couple had already booked into the hotel. Perhaps they hadn't read all the joining information on the letter and hadn't realised they also needed to register with her at the temporary Super Sun desk.

Through the archway into the lobby, Fiona noticed a couple approaching the small table covered in flyers for tourist attractions within reach of the hotel. Any hopes she had that they might be her missing passengers were quickly dashed when she realised that although the man, with his thinning grey hair could well be the right sort of age, the person with him was only a teenager. The girl had her back to Fiona. She was small, about four feet ten inches tall, and her long dark-brown hair hung freely almost to her waist. He was wearing a rucksack on his back and she had a voluminous tapestry bag slung casually over one shoulder. If they were hotel guests, they must have checked in earlier as there was no evidence of a suitcase.

Fiona decided to wait no longer. She would have to leave a message for the latecomers at the reception desk. She stood up and moved to the free-standing banner that displayed a large yellow sunburst with the words "Super Sun Executive Travel, Specialists in Luxury Short Breaks and Continental Tours" in large letters beneath.

Before she had time to collapse the stand, she noticed that the man was walking towards her with a broad smile.

'Are we late? Sorry to keep you waiting. David and Beryl Cox.' He had a strong North East accent. Not Newcastle, she decided, probably somewhere in Northumberland. She would have to check his address later.

'Not at all. It's not a problem. I'm Fiona Mason. I'm going to be your tour manager on the trip.'

They shook hands.

He looked over his shoulder and called out impatiently, 'Beryl.'

'Coming.' Clutching a fistful of brochures, the girl turned and came towards them. Her dark straight fringe accentuated the roundness of her face. It was only as she got much closer that Fiona could appreciate the age lines and that, like her husband, the woman was probably in her early sixties. The lack of height, long hair and slim lithe figure were deceiving from a distance.

'We meant to be back here a lot sooner, but we got a bit carried away, I'm afraid, didn't we, pet.' David gave Fiona an apologetic grimace. 'It took a lot longer to walk back from the cathedral than we realised.'

Fiona ticked the couple off her list and handed over their

joining envelope. Once she'd explained where to find the room for the pre-tour get-together and sent the couple on their way, she gathered her things and went to check the evening's arrangements with the hotel staff.

She had less than ten minutes to get out of her uniform and into something more comfortable if she was going to be down in time to welcome her passengers to the get-together. No time for a shower. She pulled a dress from the wardrobe, ran a brush through her hair, put a quick dab of powder on her nose – she'd never bothered much with makeup except for grand occasions and, heaven knows, there had been few enough of those in the last ten years or so – and slid her feet into a pair of comfortable low-heeled shoes.

She was about to dash out of the room when she remembered her name badge. Although, having now met them all when they'd signed in, her clients should now be able to recognise her, it might be sensible to put it on. Her uniform jacket was still lying on the bed, the badge still pinned to her lapel. As she stood fiddling with the clasp, it occurred to her that, late as it was, perhaps she should hang up the suit after all. The maid would be in to turn back her bed so best to leave the room tidy.

Bypassing the lift, she hurried down three double flights of stairs. In her experience, waiting for lifts, particularly at this busy time in the evening, was likely to take some time.

She reached the room just as Mr and Mrs Mullins turned into the corridor. Fiona smiled at the older couple and waited for them to join her.

'Are we too early?' Irene's voice was querulous. The woman still had the anxious-to-please air about her that Fiona had noticed when the couple had checked in.

'Not at all.' Fiona gave her a beaming smile. 'You look very nice.'

Though the silky, plum coloured dress had too many flounces for Fiona's taste, it was obvious the woman had made a considerable effort.

'It's not too much, is it?'

'It's perfect.'

'It did say in our letter that it was a cocktail party.'

'Exactly.' Fiona pushed the door and held it open for them. 'Let's go in.'

The two waitresses picked up their trays the moment they saw the first guests arriving.

Irene Mullins accepted a glass of sparkling white wine and her husband took a glass of fruit punch. Never much of a drinker, Fiona made it a rule never to drink alcohol on a tour and stuck with orange juice. She also declined the tray of canapés proffered by the second waitress.

'Do you have a nice room?' she asked the couple.

'It's amazing, Fiona. It's enormous and it even has a spa bath.' Irene gave a little giggle.

'Every room is different, so I understand. Have you two come far?'

'Not really. We live in Leicester and we came up by train,' answered Norman Mullins. 'We thought we'd probably have to change at Birmingham which would've taken most of the day, but we were able to get a direct train that got us here just after lunch.'

'I don't suppose that gave you much of a chance to look round Liverpool, did it?'

'No. Not really.' Norman shook his head. 'By the time we'd checked in and had a bite to eat, we only had a couple of hours or so. We did walk down to the river and along by those lovely buildings. The one with the famous bird statues on top.'

'The Royal Liver Building,' said Fiona. 'I expect you've heard the story about the birds, haven't you?'

Irene shook her head.

'The one at the front facing onto the Mersey is the female. She is craning her neck for a glimpse of her mate as she waits anxiously for his return from the sea, while her husband stands on the dome on the far side of the building, peering over the city trying to see if the pubs are open yet.'

From the laughter behind her, Fiona realised that two more couples had come into the room.

'That's a good one, Fiona.' Beryl Cox's voice was thin and reedy. 'Do you know what sort of birds they are supposed to be?'

'Looks a bit like a shag or a cormorant to me,' answered Joan Fletcher. She and her husband were the other couple who had just arrived. 'Greg could probably tell you. He's a bit of a bird fanatic.'

Greg Fletcher, the only one in the group with a beard, raised his eyebrows. 'Hardly! As I understand it, they're mythical creatures. The symbol of the city.'

'Do you remember that programme on the telly called *The Liver Birds*, about those two girls sharing a flat? It was way back in the 70s,' asked Irene, enthusiastically.

'Oh, yes!' Beryl clapped her hands. 'I loved it. Never missed an episode. My favourite was Polly James's character, even if she was the common one.'

'Just like you then,' said her husband with a grin.

'Thank you, darling!' Beryl pulled a face and gave David a dig in the chest with her elbow.

'They don't make those good old sitcoms like they used to,' said Greg.

Fiona left the three couples animatedly discussing the relative merits of *The Likely Lads, 'Allo 'Allo, Only Fools and Horses, Porridge* and *Dad's Army,* and moved on to a couple of younger people who were hovering by the drinks table.

'Hello, it's Stephanie, isn't it?' she asked the pretty woman who had an enviable mass of chestnut curls falling to her shoulders.

'That's right.'

Fiona turned to the man standing next to her and with a slight frown, asked tentatively, 'And you are Douglas?'

The man gave a shy smile and shook his head.

'Then it must be Chester. I can tell I'm going to have difficulty telling you two apart.' She looked around. 'There's Douglas talking with Louise and Greg. Have you two met them yet?'

She would have no difficulty recognising Colin, who wore glasses, and his pretty fair-haired wife who was probably the youngest member of the group.

Stephanie and Chester shook their heads. 'Then let me introduce you.'

Trying to make conversation with the younger members of the party was proving a little more difficult than with the older ones. 'Have any of you been up to the terrace bar at the very top of the building?'

'Oh yes,' Douglas Redhill answered, a smile lighting up his face. 'It's a magnificent view, isn't it?'

'We haven't been up there yet, but we have got an excellent view from our bedroom window, haven't we, Colin?' said Louise Davenport.

'You'll get a chance when we go up for dinner,' Fiona assured her.

After half an hour, Fiona had had a chance to wander around and exchange a few words with each of her passengers. She discovered that the majority had taken up the company offer to book at least one extra night to spend more time seeing the sights of Liverpool. The exceptions were the Davenports, the young couple from nearby Manchester who knew the city well, and Douglas Redhill from a village just south of Ellesmere Port, who had even less distance to travel. Most of her passengers lived relatively near, either in the North or the Midlands, which was probably one of the reasons for choosing the holiday. However attractive the final destination, a long, difficult journey at the start and finish of a tour could act as a major deterrent. The Fletchers, Greg and Joan had the longest journey and had travelled up the day before from St Austell in Cornwall, even further than Fiona, whose hometown was Guildford in Surrey. It had taken all day, two changes, and over seven hours on the train, for the Fletchers to get to Liverpool. At least, once she'd reached London, Fiona had been whisked up by a fast, direct train in only just over three hours.

Fiona picked up a spoon from the side table and gently tapped her glass to attract everyone's attention. 'I appreciate that I've spoken to each of you already, but I would like to officially welcome you all to the Super Sun "Beautiful Belfast and Northern Ireland Tour". You all have your information packs and have a detailed itinerary of what we will be doing for the next eight days, but, if you have any questions at any time, please ask and I'll do my best to help. That's what I'm here for. I do hope you have all had a chance to meet your fellow travellers, but we can carry on getting to know one another over dinner. If you would like to follow me, I will lead you to the restaurant and show you the tables that have been reserved for us all.'

By the time she got to her room that evening, Fiona was surprisingly tired. True, she'd spent her morning in the Maritime Museum, but for most of the afternoon, she'd sat doing nothing but wait for her passengers to check in.

This was the first tour where there had been an introductory get-together. To call it a cocktail party was overstating it, but everyone had appeared to enjoy themselves. It had been an excellent opportunity to get to know everyone.

Now she'd had a chance to exchange a few words with everyone, thankfully there appeared perfectly amiable and friendly. She had the feeling that she might need to look after the oldest couple, the Mullinses, who seemed to be in need of reassurance and there were three single passengers she would need to ensure didn't feel left out. At least there were no awkward customers who stood out and she'd certainly had her share of those in the past. The only problem she could foresee so far was going to be distinguishing between her two single male passengers. Both were in their late thirties, around the same height with medium brown hair. Chester Porter had a rounder face than

Douglas Redhill, but from the back, it was difficult to tell which was which. Douglas didn't seem quite so reserved as Chester who, though not one for small talk, nonetheless had a ready smile.

Time to phone her boys. Martin was never one to go to bed early, but it made sense to phone him first.

'Hi, Mum. How goes it? Did you enjoy Liverpool?'

Unlike her eldest son, who never seemed to remember her tour plans, Martin never had a problem recalling what she'd told him the previous Sunday. Perhaps it was Adam's way of showing his disapproval of her working as a tour manager at all. Even though she'd been doing the job for well over a year now, he still insisted that she must take care not to do too much and overtax herself.

'Very much, thank you, darling. Though even with two whole days and no passengers to worry about, I only managed to skim the surface of all there is to see.'

'Have you met all your passengers yet?'

'Oh yes. We've just had a get-together party. They all seem perfectly pleasant. Four couples and three travelling alone. Quite a mixed group really. Apart from an older couple in their late seventies, most of them are relatively young, several in their late thirties, early forties which is rather unusual for coach tours. Still, I suppose this is a little bit different to the continental itineraries that I'm usually offered.'

Martin laughed. 'You don't need a passport for a start.'

'That's true. This is a new tour and a bit of an experiment on the company's part so it will be interesting to see how well it goes. One good thing is that it will involve considerably less travelling to get there than some I've had in the past.'

'That can't be a bad thing.'

'Too true! Having to spend the best part of the first couple of days sitting on the coach to get to our destination never brings out the best in people. It will also make a pleasant change to be able to stay in the same hotel for the whole week once we arrive in Belfast without having to constantly think about packing and unpacking. Now, what have you been up to this week? Anything exciting?'

Day 2 Monday

This morning we head for the Twelve Quays Terminal in Birkenhead to catch the mid-morning ferry to Belfast. We will arrive at the Victoria Terminal 2 in the early evening.

As we sail up Belfast Lough, you will be greeted by two iconic landmarks standing on the dockside – the architectural splendour of Titanic Belfast, the world's largest Titanic visitor experience, and two great yellow cranes known as Samson and Goliath.

Titanic Belfast lies alongside the Harland and Wolff yards where the great ship was built. Designed to resemble the shape of ships' prows, the building was constructed in 2012 to celebrate the centenary of RMS Titanic's maiden voyage.

The two giant Harland and Wolff gantry cranes towering over the Titanic Quarter, were built in 1969 and 1974 and at that time, were the largest ever built. Sampson and Goliath stand 95m and 106m high and are still in use today.

Our hotel for our stay in Northern Ireland is the Belfast Hilton. This magnificent five-star hotel is located on the banks of the river Lagan and is only a two-minute walk from the city centre.
Super Sun Executive Travel

Two

Fiona hummed to herself as she slipped her feet into her navy court shoes and turned to the long mirror to check that she looked presentable. She smoothed her hands down the hips of her straight uniform skirt. It was a lot tighter than it had been this time last year. Perhaps that was a good thing. She had lost so much weight in the final years of Bill's illness and the immediate aftermath of his death that she knew that friends and family had worried about her. Whatever Adam might say, this job was good for her. It had had its moments; that was certainly true. She had to admit, it was far from stress-free, but it was good to get away from the confines of the bungalow to which she'd been tied for so long, and to see places she would otherwise probably never visit. Most of her passengers were a joy to look after. Plus, she wasn't ready to sit back and do nothing. She needed to feel useful.

It wasn't just the thought of a new and interesting itinerary that put her in a good mood. She was looking forward to catching up with Winston. She'd only had the briefest of chats with her West Indian driver when he had arrived with the coach mid-afternoon on the previous day. He had come to find her at her station off the lobby. Knowing she would be busy with the arriving guests for the rest of the day, they arranged to meet for breakfast in the morning.

It seemed a long time since she'd seen him. Her previous tour was just over a month ago. Fiona was one of the few part-time tour managers in the company. Most worked full time with just four or five days at home between tours. She had made it clear from the outset that she would prefer to do only one tour a month, but, after a particularly stressful tour to Berlin and the Elbe Valley at Easter, she had taken a longer break than usual. Their seven-day trip to Paris and Normandy in early May had been a joy: cheerful, co-operative passengers, interesting places to visit and warm, sunny weather. With luck, this trip would prove to be just as enjoyable.

Winston was already sitting at a small table in the corner when she reached the restaurant. He rose to his feet as she crossed the room towards him. Towering above her, he embraced her in a quick hug, burying her in his massive chest.

'How is you, sweetheart?'

'All the better for seeing you.'

For five minutes, they exchanged pleasantries and updated each other on their respective families. Fiona recounted the latest exploits of her two grandchildren, Becky, now six and Adam Junior who was keeping Adam and his wife, Kristie, on their toes as he went through the "terrible twos". In the few odd days, he was back in England between tours, Winston lived with his mother in Islington and recently his sister had moved back in with her two daughters.

'So how did the get-together go last night?'

'Fine. All the passengers seem pleasant.'

'So, no troublemakers.'

'No,' she said tentatively, picking up the teapot and pouring herself a cup. 'No obvious complainers anyway. Not that much has happened for them to start moaning about yet.'

'You don't sound so sure.'

'It's just that half the group appear to be in their thirties.'

Winston raised an eyebrow. 'That's different, but I can't see why it's a problem.'

'I'm keeping my fingers crossed that they don't split into two separate groups. With only eleven passengers, it's even more important everyone gets on.'

'Why do you think we have so few?'

'I suppose it could be because it is a comparatively pricey tour. Small group tours are obviously more costly, but this is the most expensive of all the short breaks in the brochure. Hotels in any capital city are always expensive and, I suppose, unlike cities such as Paris where we get a discount for multiple bookings for tours heading further into France and the rest of Europe, it's not as if Super Sun will be returning to Belfast on the way to anywhere else.'

'It's a brand-new tour as well. Some new tours have to run a few times before the numbers pick up.'

'True. I know many people, especially the older ones opt for tours that have been recommended by friends, so let's hope this tour is a success and it will prove more popular in future. I'm looking forward to it anyway. The itinerary looks great.'

'You bin here before?' he asked.

Fiona shook her head. 'No. Have you?'

'Nope.'

'Well,' Fiona pursed her lips in a look of mock disapproval. 'That's not on, Mr Taylor! You know how much I rely on you for your local knowledge.'

Winston's deep rumbling chuckle resounded through their section of the room. 'I think we'll cope, sweetheart. We always do. And you needn't worry about today. There's not much for you to do. It's straight to the ferry and then we'll be spending the whole day on board then a short hop to the hotel in time for dinner.'

'Eight hours! I was surprised when I saw it would take so long to cross the Irish Sea. But then Belfast is some way north of Liverpool, and we do have to go right round the Isle of Man.'

Winston spread butter onto a slice of toast then looked across at her. 'You not going to treat yourself to a cooked breakfast, sweetheart? Don't suppose the food will be up to Super Sun standard on the ferry.'

'I was going to,' she said, wistfully, 'but my uniform is telling me to watch my weight. If I don't start off being careful, I'll never be able to get into this skirt on the day we travel back.'

'Well, I ain't leaving here till I see you eat a proper breakfast, so get yourself over to that buffet table before I get cross.'

Fiona chuckled. 'You never get cross.'

'There's always a first time, sweetheart.'

Still laughing, Fiona made her way across the room to the large covered silver trays. The idea of an angry Winston was as difficult to imagine as a politician keeping his promise.

At the buffet table, she found herself standing next to another of her passengers. If their brief conversation the previous evening was anything to go by, Fiona decided Chester Porter was the quiet retiring type.

'Good morning, Fiona.'

He had already loaded his plate and now headed back in the main body of the rapidly filling restaurant. She watched him return to his seat. She didn't like to think he would be having a solitary breakfast, but she needn't have worried. He joined Colin and Louise Davenport, the pleasant out-going young couple, and another of the single passengers, Stephanie Jessen. That was the advantage of last night's cocktail party; everyone was already getting to know one another.

Montgomery-Jones stood at the window of his office high on an upper floor of Vauxhall Cross, overlooking the river Thames. He took the antique hunter watch that had once belonged to his grandfather from his waistcoat pocket and glanced at the time before replacing it and readjusting its chain over the striped regimental tie. His expression remained impassive. A knock at the door broke his reverie.

'Come in.'

James Fitzwilliam opened the door and stood back to allow a second man to enter. 'Mr Salmon for you, sir.'

As the door closed softly behind him, Andrew Salmon walked forward, holding out his hand. 'Good morning, Peter. Thank you for making time to see me.'

The two men shook hands and Montgomery-Jones gestured his guest to one of the easy chairs. 'And to what do I owe the pleasure of a visit from MI5? Can I assume it has something to do with the Eamon McCollum case?'

Salmon unbuttoned his jacket and sat back in the chair, crossing one leg over the other. 'That's what I like about you, Peter. Always straight to the point.' Despite his attempt to affect a casual air of bonhomie, Salmon appeared ill at ease. Not an uncommon reaction among those who came into the presence of the solemn, somewhat imperious, silver-haired MI6 chief. Montgomery-Jones was always impeccably dressed in a three-piece Saville Row suit and had an accent that spoke of Eton, Oxford, and Sandhurst.

'I won't deny it,' Salmon hurried on. 'But this conversation is off the record. I don't mind telling you, I'm worried. You remember what happened last time we thought we had him?'

'As I recall, the prosecution case fell through when one witness was killed in a hit-and-run two weeks before the trial and the other two suddenly refused to testify.'

'That's right. This situation is completely different. The bomb-making equipment was found on McCollum's property, but...' Salmon's voice tailed off and he shrugged his shoulders.

'You believe that the likelihood is that McCollum will claim that he knew nothing about it.'

'Exactly that. He's adamant that he's been set up, either by the Police Service or one of the Ulster loyalist paramilitary groups. We were hoping that forensics would be able to disprove that, but unfortunately, he was too clever to physically handle any of the arms equipment himself. Not that that negates the case for McCollum overseeing the operation of course.'

'This is surely a matter for the Northern Ireland Police

Service. Why is MI5 involved?'

Salmon smiled. 'We have an informant inside McCollum's CIRA cell. He was the one who tipped off the police that the arms had been delivered. They were only due to be in the lockup for a few hours, so the timing of the raid was crucial.'

'Is McCollum aware of who betrayed him?'

'I very much hope not,' Salmon answered with feeling. 'My man is pretty flaky. Wants out; not surprisingly. After a great deal of cajoling, I've managed to persuade him to carry on. Apart from anything else, if he runs now, it will be all McCollum needs as proof. It would be a death sentence. The best thing for him would be to help us put McCollum behind bars for good. I've promised him that if everything goes to plan, there will be enough evidence at McCollum's trial that we won't need to reveal our source to prove McCollum's involvement.'

Both men sipped their coffees in silence for a few moments.

'Am I to take it that you wish to involve MI6 in some way?'

Salmon ran his tongue along his top lip, evidently uncomfortable with Montgomery-Jones's direct approach.

'Well, the arms are all of Russian manufacture, and MI5 is anxious to trace the supply chain. That is why we recruited an informer in the first place. As I don't need to tell you, the quantity of arms coming in to supply not just dissidents on both sides in Northern Ireland but many of the anti-establishment groups over here on the mainland is escalating to alarming proportions. The network is complex and extensive, but MI5 are no nearer to getting to the hub, which we believe is somewhere in Eastern Europe. At this stage, all I'm saying is that I'd like to pick your brains on an informal basis. I'm not asking for any official involvement in any kind of joint operation. At least not yet.'

'I see. Did you have anything specific in mind?'

Salmon sighed. 'Going back to the earlier trial, what do

you remember about the witness who was run down?'

'Very little. It was not a case where MI6 had any involvement.'

'The victim's name was Philip Masterson. A thirty-one-year-old research physicist from Leeds over in Belfast for a conference at Queen's University. He was out walking in the area late at night and was able to identify McCollum as the man issuing orders just before the bomb went off outside the police station. He came forward straight away. Not only that, he also told all his fellow attendees at the conference all about it.'

'Brave man.'

'I doubt he appreciated the consequences of shooting his mouth off so readily. Had he been in the country longer he may have been more circumspect. As you know, there was little doubt at the time that McCollum or the CIRA had him eliminated even though, as you'd expect, nothing could be proved, and the coroner eventually had to bring in a verdict of hit and run by person or persons unknown. After Masterson's death, the other two witnesses suddenly changed their statements.'

'I appreciate the history lesson, Andrew, and I can see why you are concerned for your informant, but I am still not clear what has this to do with me or MI6?'

'I'm coming to that,' Salmon said, irritably. 'Masterson had an older brother, Edward. At the inquest, Edward claimed that days before his death, Philip received threats that he would be eliminated if he didn't withdraw his evidence against McCollum. They came in the form of anonymous phone calls, so Edward could produce no evidence which meant that no action could be taken against McCollum. Edward Masterson then made very public threats that he would see justice was done. However long it took, he would do to McCollum what the man had done to his brother.'

'Yes, that I do remember. It hit the front pages of all the newspapers.'

'When McCollum was taken into custody two weeks ago, Edward Masterson repeated his threat. He posted on his Facebook page that McCollum had better keep looking over his shoulder because his time was up.'

'You are taking his threat seriously?'

'We can't afford not to.'

'I see.'

'If you hear any rumours in your territory on the Irish side of the border, we'd be grateful if you'd tip us the wink.'

Three minutes after Salmon's departure, James Fitzwilliam knocked on the door and walked in. He placed papers on the large desk. 'Good meeting, sir?'

Montgomery-Jones raised an eyebrow. 'Is that a circuitous way of asking me what it was about?'

James gave a sheepish grin. 'I am a little curious. Are we going to be involved in a joint operation?'

'I believe the words that Salmon used were wanting "to pick my brains".'

James gave a derisive snort. 'Forgive me, sir, but I find that hard to believe. MI5, and Salmon in particular, hate our guts. There must be a lot more to this than he's telling you.'

'That is putting it a little strongly, though I agree in normal circumstances, he would be somewhat reticent about involving MI6. Quite what he has in mind, we will have to wait and see what transpires.'

Three

The major difficulty with their hotel was that the original White Star offices, built in the late 1890s, were never designed to cater for the comings and goings of a large number of hotel guests at the same time. For a start, it had no car park and the entrance opened straight onto James Street, a busy thoroughfare leading down to the Pier Head and the Albert Docks. It was impossible for the coach to stop long enough outside for all the cases to be loaded. Although the hotel catered for large groups, these were mostly events such as wedding parties, at which guests did not arrive and depart en masse. Helped by one of the hotel porters, Winston had had to wheel the luggage trolley through several streets to the nearest point where he'd been able to park the coach.

Even arrangements for boarding all eleven passengers were not straightforward. The entrance lobby was small and waiting on the busy pavement outside was not practical, besides which, the Super Sun coach was a large vehicle for the modest size of James Street. Although staying in a Titanic-themed hotel set a wonderful atmosphere for the start of the trip and the rooms, food and service could not be faulted, Fiona decided that she would have to let Head Office know that on future tours staying in Liverpool, a hotel with its own car park, or at least a drop-off and pick-up area, was essential.

It was less than a two-minute walk to the pickup point that Winston had suggested and, as Fiona led the way, everyone seemed in relatively good spirits. With luck, assuming there were not too many problems in the next week, by the time they filled in their tour appraisal forms at the end of the tour, they would have forgotten about this inconvenience. She ushered them all onto the coach as quickly as was practical.

She barely had time to introduce Winston before they arrived at the Mersey tunnel. It was only a 20-minute journey to Birkenhead docks, so Fiona decided to leave explaining how to access the individual entertainment system on Super Sun's latest **Imperial-class coach** until a future time.

Fiona went out on deck to watch the ferry sail up the Mersey estuary. It was a chance to catch a last glimpse of Liverpool. To judge by the crowds two and three rows deep at the starboard rail, the majority of the other ferry passengers had had the same idea. Her attempts to peer over the shoulders of those in front were not proving to be particularly successful so she gave up. She was about to move over to the port side and see if there was anything of interest on the Birkenhead Bootle shore, when she heard someone call her name.

Colin Davenport was not only tall, he was broad shouldered with the build of a man who worked out regularly. He pushed his glasses up his nose with one finger then raised his hand in the air and waved her over.

'Room for a little one in here, Fiona.' His powerful voice rang out over the general hubbub.

He moved back a little to let her squeeze in front and gently eased her next to his wife who was already on the front row.

'I don't want to push in,' Fiona protested, but with his hand around her shoulder propelling her forward, she didn't have much choice.

The ferry was now in midstream and had already passed the Albert Docks, though looking back Fiona could just make out the Liver Building behind the white roof of the cruise ship terminal.

'I didn't realise there were so many docks. They go on for miles,' Louise Davenport said.

Louise was not much taller than Fiona, hardly reaching her husband's shoulders, but she had his ready smile. Her ash blonde hair was a similar shade to Fiona's but without the hint of white wings beginning to develop over the temples that Fiona had noticed in the mirror as she'd dried her hair that morning. Louise's hair was also much longer, and she had it tied back in a ponytail.

Soon they were heading out into the deeper waters of the Irish Sea.

'Bye bye, Liverpool.' Louise gave a cheery wave.

'It's going to be a long time before you can say, "Hello, Belfast," so you'd better decide what you want to do for the next eight hours,' said her husband. 'I hope you put lots of reading matter in that bag of yours.'

'For your information, Mr Clever, I've brought my Kindle and a pile of crosswords to do,' Louise said slipping her arm through his. 'Though I expect the time will pass quickly enough by the time we've had a bit of lunch and the odd stroll around the deck.'

Colin turned to Fiona. 'I suppose you've done this crossing several times, haven't you?'

'Actually no. This is a new tour for Super Sun this year. There's a demand for shorter and UK-based tours apparently.'

'Well it certainly suits us,' said Louise. 'We moved house a couple of months ago, and we've been so busy decorating and trying to get the garden in some sort of order ever since, that we felt in need of a break. We didn't want to be away too long either so there was no point wasting too much time travelling to wherever we decided to go.'

'We looked at a couple of the four and five day breaks to start with, but as we've never been to Ireland, we decided to opt for this,' added Colin.

'I'm sure you'll love Belfast. It is a beautiful city,' said Fiona.

'I'm looking forward to seeing the Giant's Causeway. It looks so impressive in all the pictures.'

Fiona said goodbye to the Davenports and made her way below. Time for a coffee. The Davenports were probably the youngest members of the group. Perhaps by promoting these new short breaks, Super Sun were trying to attract a younger busy working clientele. She hadn't considered that when she was chatting about the number of thirty-somethings in the group with Winston earlier.

As Louise Davenport had predicted, despite all her misgivings, the long journey passed more quickly than Fiona had feared. Over a late lunch, the older couple, Irene and Norman Mullins, invited her to sit with them. They were seasoned Super Sun travellers and once Irene had given Fiona a blow-by-blow account of their last tour to the Italian Lakes, the talkative woman proceeded to tell her all about their eldest grandchild's wedding that had taken place the previous week. Even though lunch had been only a sandwich and a cup of coffee, glancing at her watch, Fiona realised that her chat with Irene and Norman had taken well over an hour and a half.

Making her apologies, Fiona got to her feet and turned towards the exit. The ship was rolling gently in the rougher open water of the Irish Sea but was enough to make Fiona have to concentrate as she tried to time her steps to the rhythm of the ship's movement. An unexpected lurch meant she had to grab hold suddenly to the back of someone's chair. She was in the middle of apologising to the woman sitting there when a commotion at the drinks serving counter made her look up.

'Look what you're doing!'

Greg Fletcher looked as though he was about to punch Chester Porter who stood holding a paper cup, an agonised expression on his face, staring at Joan who had her back to

Fiona.

Fiona hurried over to the three of them almost at a run to prevent herself falling as the rocking motion of the ship continued. Only now could she see that the front of Joan's blouse was covered in a dark brown coffee stain that continued to expand as the liquid slowly seeped from the neckline right towards the hem.

'I am *so* sorry!'

Greg looked as though he was about to explode. 'You clumsy oaf…'

Fiona stepped quickly between the two men. 'That sudden lurch caught us all out.'

She pulled out a handy pack of tissues from her bag so that Joan could at least wipe away the coffee splashes from her face and exposed forearms.

'Let's get you to the ladies and clean you up.'

As they headed towards the toilets, Fiona wondered about the wisdom of leaving the two men alone together. It may have been an accident, but she wasn't sure that Greg was in a forgiving frame of mind. Having Chester ending up with a bloodied nose would not be the best start to their arrival in Belfast.

Four

Whatever Greg's reaction to the incident, Joan didn't appear to share her husband's grudge against Chester.

'You'll have to forgive Greg. He can have a bit of a temper on him when he gets overtired. We had a really long day on Saturday travelling up from Cornwall. It was a nightmare of a journey and he doesn't sleep well in a strange bed.'

Joan removed her sodden blouse and held it up. 'It's much too wet to put on again. Thank goodness, I brought my cardigan with me when we got out of the coach. It's far too hot to wear inside really, but I don't have any other option.'

'Give it to me while you wash yourself down. If you're not going to wear it now, shall I run it under the cold tap? At least we can try and get the coffee out before it ruins your blouse altogether. Then we'll have to see if we can get a plastic bag to put it in. Perhaps the shop will help.'

'Thank you, Fiona. That would be great. The coffee soaked right down to my trousers. The waistband is all wet and there are splashes all down the legs. Oh well,' Joan said shaking her head, 'There's not much I can do about that now. I'll have to wait until we get to the hotel and I get my case.'

By the time the two women returned to the café area, the place was half empty. Most people had probably decided to go up on deck to catch sight of land. Greg was sitting at one of the tables facing the door, scratching at his beard, his eyes hooded. He was not a happy man. He got to his feet and walked towards them. Fiona looked around, but Chester was nowhere to be seen. She wasn't sure if that was a good or a bad thing. Judging from the grim expression on Greg's face, the parting of the two men had not been amicable. Best not to ask if he knew where Chester had gone.

Fiona decided to leave Joan and Greg alone and trust that Joan could talk some sense into her husband. There was no point in her trying to find Chester. It would not be too long before the ship's tannoy would be announcing that it was time for passengers to return to their vehicles. Fiona made her way up to the deck.

The ferry terminal was barely half a mile into Belfast Lough. Fiona decided that the spectacular views of the Belfast Titanic, promised in the Super Sun literature were well overstated. The building was a good three miles downriver, though it probably didn't help that the late afternoon was dull with low cloud. Fiona made a mental note to put it in her notes for Head Office. Best not to give future difficult passengers any ammunition by making false claims.

Fiona always tried to ensure that she was one of the first to arrive down on the car deck when they travelled by ferry but, even though no vehicles would be allowed to move until all the docking procedures were complete which always took some time, the stairways were always packed with people racing to get back to the cars.

When she reached the coach, Greg, Joan and Stephanie were already sitting in their seats. The others began to arrive soon after. News of what had happened did not appear to have filtered through although when Chester arrived with the tail-enders, one or two passengers turned to stare at his pale, withdrawn face as he squeezed his way down the narrow aisle to a seat right at the back of the coach.

The Belfast Hilton was only a short journey from the terminal. If the Super Sun literature had failed on its details about their approach to Belfast, there could be no complaints about its plaudits for their hotel. Not only did it live up to its five-star rating, it was modern and spacious, bright and welcoming. Its location was ideal, with magnificent views over the river on one side and the city on the other. If their evening meal matched the standard Fiona had seen so far, they were in for an excellent stay.

It didn't escape her notice that when she asked everyone to take a seat while she checked them in and collected their keys from reception, Chester hung back hovering a few feet away. He was still standing there, half hidden behind a pillar, by the time she returned.

'Dinner tonight will be at eight o'clock in the main restaurant and once I've given you your keys you can go straight up to your rooms. Winston is already unloading the main cases so it shouldn't be too long before they're delivered to your rooms.'

She was tempted to keep Chester's key till last so she could check that he was okay but decided it might be best to leave well alone and hope that the whole unfortunate episode would blow over.

When all her passengers had disappeared, she turned back to the entrance and went to check the line of cases. Hers still wasn't there so she waited for Winston to unload the last few pieces of luggage.

'That's the lot, sweetheart.'

'Thanks, Winston. I'll take mine up myself.' She pulled up the handle on her case and was about to head for the lifts when Winston called her back.

'Anything wrong, sweetheart? You look done in.'

She gave him a weak smile. 'Let's just say, I'll be glad to get to my room. There was a bit of an incident on the ferry just before we landed.'

'Oh?'

'Did you notice the ship gave a sudden lurch at one point?'

Winston nodded and she quickly filled him in on what had happened. 'It was an accident of course but Joan's husband was furious. At one point, I thought it would come to blows.'

Winston clamped a hand on her shoulder and gave it a squeeze. 'Don't worry about it, sweetheart. They'll forget about it soon enough.'

Greg and Joan were already standing outside the restaurant by the time Fiona got there. They were deep in conversation with David and Beryl Cox. She couldn't hear what he was saying but from the earnest tone in his voice, it was clear that Greg was already giving them his version of what had happened.

'If you four would like to go in, our tables are over by the window. You'll be able to tell which ones by the little Super Sun flag in the centre.'

The last thing she needed was Greg stirring it with more people than necessary so best to limit the damage and send them in before anyone else arrived.

She wondered if Chester would come down to eat at all after the way Greg had been glaring at him while the keys were being given out, but he arrived almost at the same time as Colin and Louise Davenport. The four of them went into the restaurant together and sat down at the last of the three tables that had been reserved for them.

Although Chester was never much of a talker, throughout the first two courses, he was virtually monosyllabic. Thank goodness, typical outgoing Northerners, Colin and Louise kept the conversation going throughout the meal.

'What's that big circular building next door to the hotel, Fiona? Is it the theatre?' Colin asked.

'That's right. The Belfast Waterfront puts on all sorts of shows as well as classical and rock concerts, opera and ballet. But the building isn't just a theatre. It holds all sorts of exhibitions and it's a major conference centre. And I believe I'm right in saying, you can even get married there.'

'Depending what's on this week, as it's right next door, it might be a good opportunity to go to a performance one evening. What do you think, Louise?' Colin asked.

'Sure. Though we may need to eat a lot earlier or later, depending on what time the programme starts.'

'That's true. But we need to see what's on first.'

'I expect you'll find a flyer at the front desk. I remember seeing the hotel had all sorts of information about local attractions for guests,' said Fiona.

Turning to Chester, Fiona tried to draw him into the conversation. 'What about you? Are you a theatre-goer, Chester?'

'I prefer live theatre to the cinema.'

'Do you get much opportunity where you live? Does Leeds have any decent theatres?'

Chester managed a genuine smile and nodded. 'We've a large modern repertory theatre and The Grand which is an old Victorian building.'

'Isn't that where Opera North is based?' Louise asked.

Chester nodded. 'They're incredibly good.'

'We're very well served in Manchester,' Louise continued. 'Apart from the Palace and the Exchange, we've got the Opera house. We love a good musical.'

As she recounted various recent shows she and Colin had seen, Fiona could cast an eye over the rest of her passengers. Greg was still holding forth and she noticed Beryl turn her head to look over at Chester with a decidedly disapproving stare. It was bad enough Greg still bearing a grudge without him trying to persuade other passengers to ostracise Chester.

Day 3 Tuesday

Our day begins with a panoramic drive around Belfast. As we tour the city's centre, we will be able to appreciate Belfast's many fine buildings including the City Hall, the Albert Memorial Clock and the Grand Opera House.

Although Belfast is now a peaceful city, we all know of its turbulent history. During the Troubles from 1969 to 1998, the gable ends of some Belfast homes were decorated to show their owner's political affiliations. We will see many of these as we pass down the Protestant Shankill Road and the Catholic Falls Road.

Next, we will journey south to Queen's University. This attractive Tudor-style red brick and honey-coloured sandstone building was designed by Charles Lanyon in 1849. The university was founded by Queen Victoria in 1845 as one of three Queen's colleges intended to provide non-denominational education. At that time, the University of Dublin was only open to Anglicans. Our guided tour will take us to the university's Great Hall, the Canada Room and the School of Music.

The university borders the Botanic Gardens and after our tour of the building, we will visit the gardens and see the magnificent glass Palm House. The Belfast Botanic and Horticultural Society established the gardens in 1828. Its most noticeable feature is the Palm House with its birdcage dome, a superb structure of cast iron and curved glass panels, dating from 1839. As well as banana and cinnamon trees, bromeliads and orchids, the Palm House contains hanging baskets, seasonal displays and birds of paradise. It also holds some of the oldest surviving seed plants.

After lunch, we will travel a short distance east of the city to see Stormont, the seat of the Northern Ireland Assembly. Built to house Northern Ireland's parliament between 1928 and 1932, this magnificent Anglo-Palladian building is constructed of Portland stone and Mourne granite. After the government was disbanded in 1972, it was used as government offices, but since the 1998 Agreement, it has become home to the devolved Northern Ireland Assembly.

Finally, we will return to the city centre and head north to Cave Hill and Belfast Castle. The castle stands on the wooded eastern slopes of the hill. Built in 1870, it was the home of the Earl of Shaftesbury although it now belongs to the city. Here we will have a short photo stop where we will enjoy the splendid views over Belfast Lough and the city below.
Super Sun Executive Travel

Five

'I'll drive back to the car park by the university at two o'clock to pick you all up and then we can head on over to Stormont,' said Winston.

'Assuming everything goes to plan, that should give everyone a couple of hours to wander round the Botanical Gardens, take a look in the Palm House and find themselves somewhere to have lunch.' Fiona glanced out of the window. 'And, by the look of it, we have a lovely day for it. Gardens always look so much nicer when the sun is shining.'

'Doesn't everything?'

'You're right, Winston. Of course, it does.'

'The weather forecast is good for most of the next week. Possibility of a few showers on Saturday.'

'That's the day we visit Mount Stewart house. Let's hope they don't amount to much.'

Fiona poured herself a second cup of tea.

'After that delicious sticky toffee pudding with butterscotch sauce and ice cream after an enormous plate of Irish lamb that we ate at dinner last night, I shouldn't be contemplating breakfast at all. But I must confess, the smell of that bacon wafting over from the table behind us is making my mouth water at the thought of a bacon roll.'

'Why not, sweetheart? That tiny bowl of fruit isn't going to get you through till lunch time.' Winston pushed back his chair and got to his feet. 'I'm off. I'll bring the coach round to the entrance for nine o'clock.'

'Wonderful. See you then. I'll make sure we're all ready

and waiting. That's another great thing about this tour.' She looked up at him with a grin. 'No early morning starts.'

The restaurant was filling up fast by the time Fiona returned to her table. She noticed Chester standing nearby looking in vain for an empty table. He looked considerably less tense than last evening; perhaps like her, he'd decided to put yesterday's mishap and its unfortunate aftermath behind him.

'There's a seat here if you don't mind sharing with me.'

He gave her a grateful smile. 'Of course not, Fiona. It's always a little tricky when you're on your own. You don't like to intrude on strangers.'

That was one way of putting it. She was well aware that what he really meant was that he was not sure what kind of reception he might receive from some of his fellow passengers. Deciding to take his words at face value, she said, 'I know what you mean. Somehow, it's not so bad if there are two of you. When there's just one, other people somehow feel obliged to make conversation with you, which can be a little embarrassing.'

'Exactly.'

'Well, I'm not a stranger.' They both laughed. 'As you know, you are not the only single passenger on the trip. Have you had a chance to talk with the other two?'

'I sat with Stephanie at breakfast yesterday, though apart from a few words with Douglas at the cocktail party, I can't say we've had a real conversation.'

'It's still early days. So, tell me, what made you choose to come to Belfast?'

'I've never been to Ireland, North or South, but I suppose the deciding factor was seeing the Super Sun advert in the travel section in the Sunday Times with a picture of the Giant's Causeway. It's always been somewhere I dearly wanted to see. Geology was one of my passions when I was a boy. My bedroom was full of fossils and rock samples, much to my mother's annoyance – she said they created dust all over the place. I begged my parents to take me on holiday there, but it never happened. When I saw that photo with the sun dropping into the sea over those amazingly shaped rocks, I picked up the phone there and then and booked it.' He gave an embarrassed laugh. 'You could say it was a sudden impulse.'

Half an hour later, as she made her way back up to her room, Fiona made a mental note to keep an eye on Chester, to make sure he wasn't left out. Even without yesterday's incident, he was so self-effacing. After his burst of enthusiasm over the Giant's Causeway, it had been hard work making social chitchat over breakfast. However, she had managed to prise out of him that he was a software engineer, his parents lived down south in Bournemouth which is where he was born and brought up before moving to the north Midlands to work after university.

Greg and Joan were among the first to arrive as they gathered in the lobby ready for the tour. Chester might be doing his best to forget about yesterday, but from the way Greg glared at him, Fiona was not sure that the same could be said of him. Anyone would think, his wife had been injured the way Greg was holding a grudge. Best to take his mind off it.

'Greg, I wonder if you would do me a favour. During the walking parts of the tour, when I'm leading the way at the front, it's always a great help to me to have someone bringing up the rear to make sure we don't lose anyone, especially when we're in crowded places. I always ask the tallest person in the group. So, if you'd be kind enough to act as back marker, if I can see you, I'll know I've got everyone.'

'No problem.'

'You're a star.'

With a self-satisfied smile, he put his shoulders back and drew himself up to full height. A little flattery had worked wonders and it might even take his mind off whingeing on about Chester for a while.

Fiona did a quick head count and gathered everyone together.

'If you've already looked at your tour booklets, you'll know that tomorrow morning we'll be taking a walking tour of the city centre so we will be able to go inside many of the buildings we'll be passing on our panoramic drive. Here's the coach now, so let's go.'

Once she'd pointed out the major sites in the city centre, the coach headed east to the Falls Road.

'One of the most famous of the murals is the 'Bobby Sands memorial.'

'Wasn't he the one who went on hunger strike?' asked Beryl Cox.

'That's right. He was a member of the Provisional IRA and he initiated the hunger strike in the Maze prison in protest against the removal of the special category status. He and the other protesters demanded to be treated as political prisoners as opposed to being considered criminals. Bobby Sands died in 1981 after 66 days of refusing food. There were nine others who went on hunger strike and died a few months after each other so as to keep up the attention on their cause.'

'If you ask me,' muttered David Cox, in the seat behind Fiona, 'the picture looks more like a woman with that long hair.'

His wife shushed him with a giggle.

'Now we're going to see the murals on the Shankhill Road. Between the two areas, we'll see one of the famous Peace Lines separating this Catholic part of the city from the Protestant sector to the north. These grim-looking barriers have also been painted since the end of the Troubles with various more hopeful messages proposing peace and a coming together.'

As they drove away from the Victorian-era Crumlin Road

Gaol and headed south towards Queen's University, Fiona felt a sense of relief. One could hardly organise a tour of Belfast and ignore the past, but politics was always an area best avoided. Feelings could run high about such matters, and the last thing she needed was one of the passengers wanting to air their views on the rights and wrongs of what had happened and causing hostility with others who took the opposing view.

When they reached the university, they left the coach and Fiona led the party to the front towards the visitors' entrance passing by the Lanyon building.

'This is one of the oldest buildings on the campus which opened in 1849 making it one of the oldest universities in the United Kingdom.'

Now Fiona could relax for the next forty-five minutes and hand over to someone else to do the talking. She could leave giving any more information about the university buildings and its history to their student guide.

Six

At the end of their tour, Fiona ushered everyone outside. For some reason, there was a short holdup as they left the building. She couldn't see what the problem was and had visions of the group getting separated in the crowd of tourists milling around by the time she got there.

To her relief, most of the group had already gathered. She pulled her guide pole from her bag, extended the collapsible handle and once she'd unfurled the white flag with its Super Sun logo and held it aloft, the stragglers soon joined her.

'If you'd all like to keep together and follow me, we're going to cross over into the Botanical Gardens.'

She brought the group to a stop in front of the Palm House.

'Before I leave you all to take a look around for yourselves, I just wanted to point out that this impressive glasshouse was also designed by Sir Charles Lanyon, the same architect who, as we've just heard, designed the Queen's University building. In fact, Lanyon was responsible for designing several of the important buildings in the city including the Crumlin Road Gaol and Courthouse that we passed earlier this morning. Although this imposing glasshouse is closed for lunch at the moment, it will be open again at one o'clock.

'Is there a charge for going in the Palm House?' asked Irene Mullins.

Fiona shook her head. 'No. It's free. Now if you'd all like to look over in that direction. Can you see that massive redbrick greenhouse? It's known as the Tropical Ravine and that's also well worth a look. It was built in 1889 and it has an iron walkway which looks down on a sunken jungle of tropical ferns, orchids, lilies and bananas. Just beyond the Tropical Ravine, if you keep going in the same direction, you'll come to the Ulster Museum. It's not huge but it tells the story of the people of the north of Ireland from earliest times to the present day. There are some excellent displays that cover the two major industries which brought great wealth to Belfast, namely linen production and shipbuilding. That is also free. Unfortunately, it's not open on Tuesdays but, it might be something you'd like to think about when you have some free time to explore the city later in the week. I appreciate that most of you are intending to go and find yourself somewhere for lunch, but in the meantime, you are free to take a stroll around the gardens. Finally, ladies and gentlemen, I'll meet you all here at this spot at two o'clock. Have a lovely time, everyone.'

As they wandered off, mostly in twos or small groups, Stephanie remained a short distance away searching through the bottom of her overstuffed shoulder bag, trying not to spill any of its contents on the ground.

'Have you lost something, Stephanie?'

'I was just looking for the city map you gave us earlier. Either I've left it on the coach, or I've dropped it somewhere.'

'Not to worry. I've probably got a few spares in my bag.'

Fiona had already slipped the straps of the tote bag from her shoulder when Stephanie gave a cry of triumph.

'No, it's okay, Fiona. I've found it. Thanks anyway.'

With the folded map in one hand, Stephanie struggled to zip up the overfull bag and, in the process, the ends of her silk gauze scarf became caught.

'Here, let me help.'

Between the two of them, they managed to extract the green patterned scarf without damaging it.

'Thanks, Fiona.'

'No problem. It would be such a shame to tear it. It's so

pretty and that colour suits you so well.'

The heat and the humidity hit her as soon as she stepped through the door of the Palm House and Fiona was temporarily blinded as her sunglasses steamed over.

The path curved around the circular front. She could hear people talking ahead, though the dense foliage meant that she couldn't yet see who it was. Though the voices were so low she couldn't hear what the couple was saying, the conversation sounded strained and urgent.

As she rounded the last of the curved section, she saw Colin and Louise standing halfway along the straight stretch ahead. They didn't notice her at first, but as she approached and the couple saw her, they suddenly stopped talking.

'The flowers are lovely, aren't they?' Louise said when Fiona was a few feet from them. There was none of the usual warmth in her voice. It was all too evident they didn't want company.

'Beautiful.' Fiona smiled and squeezed past them and continued her stroll. Had she interrupted a marital tiff?

Fiona did a quick head count.

'A couple of the young people aren't here yet,' said Beryl Cox who was standing next to her.

'No problem. We've still got a few minutes.'

'There's Stephanie over there.' said David.

Fiona turned to see the athletic young woman hurrying towards the group, her shoulder length hair flying out behind her. 'No rush,' she called out.

'I'm so sorry I'm late,' Stephanie panted as she reached the group.

'You're not late. It's only just two o'clock and besides, we're still missing one person.' Fiona looked around her milling passengers. 'I think it must be Chester.'

'Isn't that him over there with his back to us, talking with Greg?'

Fiona looked at where Beryl was pointing. Even after

yesterday's fracas, she was still having difficulty identifying the two single male passengers at a distance, certainly not from behind. It didn't help that today, both men were wearing blue denim jeans and white T-shirts.

'I think that's Douglas. I'll go and check.'

By ten past two, there was still no sign of Chester Porter.

'Does anyone remember seeing him in the last couple of hours?'

'I'm pretty sure he headed off towards the museum after we all split up,' said David Cox.

'I presume he went on his own?' Fiona asked.

'Yes, I think so. Several of us set off in that direction.'

'He may have gone back to the coach already. If you'll all wait here in case he does come, I'll go and see.'

It was no more than two minutes to the coach. As she turned the corner, she could see Winston standing by the door.'

'Everything okay, sweetheart?'

'One of the passengers hasn't turned up. I came to check if he was here.'

''Fraid not, sweetheart.'

Fiona looked at her watch. 'We can't wait around much longer.'

'What do you wanna do?'

'I don't want to abandon Chester Porter all together, especially when we've only just arrived in Belfast. I suggest you drive on to Stormont with the rest of the passengers while I wait a little longer and see if he turns up. If he's not here by half past, I'll get a taxi and meet you all at the Carson Memorial. We were going to let them have twenty minutes to wander round, look at the building and take photos so that shouldn't be a problem. I'll just have to give them all the spiel about the building when I join you. It's the wrong way round I know, but at least they won't miss out.'

'Sounds good to me. Y'know, it's not exactly a rare event for passengers to go AWOL. They forget the time or get lost, and some decide they've had enough and go off and do their own thing without telling anyone. I expect when we get back to the hotel, he'll be there full of apologies. No point you getting in a tizzy about it, sweetheart.'

Fiona gave him a weak smile. 'You're right of course. I'm not worried exactly, it's just that I'd hoped to have a stress-free tour for a change.' Drawing herself up to her full five feet three inches, she said more firmly than she felt, 'Our Mr Porter is going to get a real ear-bashing from me when he does turn up.'

Seven

The taxi drew up alongside the distinctive white coach with the wavy yellow line along its side. Fiona paid the driver and went to join Winston.

'No joy, I take it?'

She sighed and shook her head. 'If he'd simply lost track of time, he should have realised by now. I gave everyone my mobile number at the start of the tour, and I remember seeing him programming it his phone. I keep checking, but he hasn't rung or left a message. It's far too early to start informing Head Office, so there's nothing more I can do right now.'

'Exactly. So, take that worried frown off your face and enjoy the rest of your afternoon, sweetheart.'

It took several minutes for everyone to get into the coach. It wasn't only the talkative Irene Mullins who was concerned about what might have happened to the missing Chester.

'Do you think he's been taken ill somewhere?' asked Beryl as she held up the others at the foot of the coach steps.

Doing her best not to seem dismissive, Fiona reassured her and gently ushered her aboard.

As she was doing a quick head count, Irene said, 'Stephanie and Douglas are still over there.'

Fiona glanced out of the window and saw the couple still deep in conversation. Douglas looked far from happy. Fiona was about to step out and call them when they both turned and hurried to the coach.

'Sorry about that.' Stephanie gave Fiona a winning smile.

Douglas mumbled an apology and head down, went to the back of the coach, thumped down onto the seat, and sat arms folded across his chest.

Fiona had far too much on her mind to bother with petty upsets and took her place so that Winston could begin the drive down the mile-long approach road back through the giant entrance pillars and onto the main road. Fiona decided that the best thing to stop any gossip and take everyone's mind off the problem was to pick up the microphone and tell everyone about their next stop.

'Now we're going to head back into the city and up to Cave Hill which is where a much earlier episode in Ireland's troubled history took place. Cave Hill stands high over the north-west tip of Belfast overlooking Belfast Lough on one side and the city to the south. This twelve-hundred-foot hill is made of basalt and it's the site of an Iron Age ring fort, the oldest settlement in the area.'

By the time she'd spun out the story of Wolfe Tone and his historic meeting in 1795 with the leaders of United Irishmen to pledge themselves to the rebellion, the coach had reached the heart of the city and they were already heading north along York Street. Everyone was busy looking out of the windows, so Fiona put down her microphone. She could wait to tell them about Belfast Castle and its history when they arrived.

She could hear Greg and Joan talking quietly in the seat behind her. Chester's name wasn't mentioned. There was nothing to suggest that his failing to return had anything to do with yesterday's incident on the ferry, but that didn't stop her wondering. Could there have been another altercation between Greg and Chester?

At the end of the day's tour, the moment the coach pulled up at the hotel, Fiona leapt down the steps hurried inside and over to the reception desk before the passengers had a chance to unbuckle their seatbelts and collect up their belongings.

'Could you tell me if Chester Porter has returned to the hotel?' In Fiona's experience, most hotel reception staff appeared to have a photographic memory for names and faces. Fiona explained her problem. 'He's one of my Super Sun party. I appreciate that with key cards, guests don't need to check in when they return, but he may have rung the hotel and left a message for me.'

The young woman Fiona spoke to had only been on duty for the last hour. She checked with her colleagues behind the desk. All three shook their heads.

'Would you like me to try his room number?'

The girl let the phone ring for what seemed an age.

'Thank you for trying. If by any chance, he does return, will you let me know straightaway? I'll give you my mobile number.'

Fiona made her way back outside. She stood back as Louise Davenport, the last of the passengers, skipped down the steps and followed her husband through the glass doors.

'Is it too soon to ring Head Office, do you think?'

'I would say so, sweetheart. Wait and see if he turns up for dinner.'

'That's what I thought you'd say.'

'No point in sitting there twiddling your thumbs for the next couple of hours. There's nothing more you can do right now so go and get yourself a nice cup of tea and forget about him for a couple of hours. Give me a buzz if there's anything I can do.'

There was a knock at the door and James entered the office with a thin manila folder in his hand. Peter Montgomery-Jones looked up from his desk.

'The report you asked for, sir. Was there anything else before I leave?'

'Thank you, Fitzwilliam. There is nothing that cannot wait until tomorrow.'

James already had his hand on the door handle when Montgomery-Jones looked up again and asked, 'Has there been any information from our Irish agents concerning possible rumours about the man MI5 are trying to track down?'

'Not a whisper, sir. I have put out a few feelers, but it has only been twenty-four hours.'

'I do appreciate it is somewhat soon to expect results. However, for Salmon to approach me, I cannot help but feel there is something more about this matter that he is not telling me.'

'Yes, sir.' James hurried out and closed the door before his boss could delay him further by asking him to chase up more contacts. He had arranged to take Laura out for the evening, and she would not be best pleased if he was held up at the office two nights in a row.

Dinner came and went. Still no word from the missing Chester Porter.

Fiona was lost in thought as she replaced her coffee cup in its saucer. 'I'm so sorry, Douglas. My mind was far away. What did you say?'

Douglas Redhill gave her a broad smile. 'I was only remarking on the fabulous view from here.'

'The view across the river is pretty special, and they have made the most of it with a whole wall of floor to ceiling windows.'

'Well if you'll all forgive me,' Douglas laid his napkin on the table and pushed back his chair. 'I'm going to love you and leave you as they say. I'm off for a gentle walk around the centre to see the city lit up.'

'That's exactly what we're planning on doing too,' said Joan.

'Just let me finish my coffee,' protested her husband.

Fiona smiled. 'I think most people are intending to take a stroll. It's such a lovely evening.'

'I know it's quite mild, but I think I'll pop up to the room and get a cardigan,' said Joan. We could be quite late coming back, especially if we call in at one of those bars that play traditional Irish music.'

'Don't let me keep you.' Fiona sat back waiting for them to disappear. Waving away the waiter advancing towards her with a pot of coffee, she too got to her feet. She couldn't put it off any longer. Time to phone Head Office. Though perhaps first she should check with the front desk and get them to phone round the hospitals.

It was evident that the girl at the night desk at Super Sun was relatively new to the job and probably had never had to deal with anything other than bookings before now.

'It's not really an emergency. I'll leave a message for the manager to look at in the morning.'

Before Fiona could insist, the girl had rung off.

It was going to be a very long night.

Day 4 Wednesday

We begin our day with a guided walk through Belfast's city centre. Our hotel is ideally situated only a few minutes' walk from Donegall Square where we will discover the impressive, newly restored Belfast City Hall, built to reflect Belfast's city status granted by Queen Victoria in 1888. It was designed by Alfred Brumwell Thomas in classical Renaissance style and completed in 1906. Its 300-foot long façade is built of Portland stone and its copper dome stands at 173 feet. Our exclusive tour of the City Hall will include the sumptuous marble and stained-glass entrance hall with its rotunda, the grand staircase, the lavish reception hall, the robes of office and the council chamber where the Northern Ireland parliament met before the building of Stormont.

In the grounds of the City Hall, we will see the Titanic Memorial erected to commemorate the lives lost in the sinking of the RMS Titanic on 15th April 1912.

The Titanic Memorial Garden was opened on the centenary of the disaster.

On our way to the Grand Opera House, we will pass the famous Crown Liquor Saloon now owned by the National Trust. The Grand Opera House is one of Belfast's great Victorian landmarks. Opened in 1895 and refurbished in the 1970s, it suffered severe bomb damage in 1991 and 1993. The magnificent interior has been restored to all its over-the-top Victorian pomp: gilt, red plush and intricate plasterwork – a tribute to the considerable skills of the Victorian craftsmen working in the city.

After our tour, there will be some free time to further explore the area. There are many excellent places to have lunch in the centre or should you choose to return to the hotel you might wish to enjoy tapas from the snack menu in the Cables Bar.

At 2 pm, we will leave the hotel for an independent visit to Titanic Belfast, which has become the most popular tourist venue in Ulster and one of the top attractions in the whole of Ireland. Opened in April 2012, this dramatic new building is located beside the Titanic Slipways, the Harland and Wolff Drawing Offices and Hamilton Graving Dock, where Titanic was designed, built and launched in 1912.

The Titanic experience will take us through nine galleries complete with sounds and smells on six floors. It tells the story of the RMS Titanic, from her conception in Belfast in the early 1900s, through her construction and launch and her famous maiden voyage to her tragic end. Aptly named, the Titanic was the biggest man-made moving object of its day. There are models showing what the ship looked like plus a re-creation of various areas of the vessel such as the 1st class cabins. The Titanic was nicknamed the "millionaire's special" because of its opulence and luxury. The great staircase in the first-class section was made famous by Kate Winslet and Leonardo DiCaprio in the film Titanic. *The tour concludes, diving to the depths of the ocean on a "virtual visit" to the wreck and her resting place on the floor of the North Atlantic.*

                          Super Sun Executive Travel

Eight

Fiona counted the seconds as she waited for the phone to be picked up at the other end. She had to consciously stop herself from drumming her fingers on the reception counter.

'I'm sorry, madam. There's no answer from Mr Porter's room.' The smartly uniformed young man behind the desk gave her an apologetic shrug of his shoulders.

Fiona mustered a smile. 'It was only a long shot.'

'I could get one of housekeeping staff to check the room.'

'Thank you. I suppose it makes sense to see if his things are still there.'

Fiona moved away from the desk and slumped down into one of the chairs by the full-length window to wait. This could take some time and there was no point in getting agitated. Best to think about something else.

'Mrs Mason?'

She hadn't heard the young man's approach. She looked up into his pale, freckled face framed with copious ginger curls.

'I'm Rory. The under-manager. Mr Porter was not in his room, Madam. It looks as though the bed has not been slept in, but his clothes are still in the wardrobe.'

Even though it was what she'd been expecting, her shoulders slumped.

Rory must have noticed because he sat in the chair facing her and asked, 'Is there anything else I can help you with?'

Fiona shook her head. She was about to get to her feet

when she changed her mind. 'Actually, it would be helpful if you would contact the police for me to let them know he is missing. I appreciate that they will only act if the missing person is a child or vulnerable person, but…'

'You need to cover all the bases,' he finished when her voice trailed off.

'Exactly.'

'No problem. We need to go through procedure too, but if you wouldn't mind hanging on here a little longer. I expect the police will want to talk to you about who saw him last, when and where.'

His soft lilting Irish brogue had a calming effect. That, and the direct way of looking straight into her eyes that made her feel she had every bit of his attention. He was young to hold such a senior position, but he was obviously very much what in today's jargon could be termed a people person.

'If you'd like to come with me, let's go into my office. It'll be a bit quieter in there.'

The next decision was whether to tell the police about the incident on the ferry. Probably not. If Chester had felt ostracised because of an unfortunate accident and decided to leave the group, he would hardly have gone without his belongings.

When she rang Head Office, she was told that David Rushworth wasn't expected in until nine o'clock. Fiona's heart sank. It wasn't unexpected, but it would have made life so much simpler if she could have spoken to the Tours Director before her walking tour was due to start. The only thing to do was to ask him to ring her as soon as possible. Letting him know the situation couldn't wait until late morning when she would be free.

Fiona took a last look round her room. She double-checked she had her mobile and that it was fully charged and switched on. She picked up a bottle of water and some spare copies of maps of Belfast, then hoisted her tote bag over her shoulder and checked her watch. She had only taken three steps down the corridor when her phone burbled.

'Mr Rushworth, thank you so much for ringing me.' Thank goodness. The man had arrived early.

She quickly brought him up to date.

'It's not unheard of for passengers to decide to leave the group for whatever reason, even without informing the tour manager, though there's usually some sort of explanation. Was he one of those difficult types, always finding fault?'

'Not at all. Quite the opposite. He was rather shy and self-effacing. All his things are still in his room which suggests he didn't decide to quit the holiday and return home.'

'And nothing else happened earlier that might explain it?'

'He was involved in an unfortunate episode over a spilt cup of coffee coming over on the ferry, but I very much doubt that had anything to do with his going missing.'

'In which case, it sounds as though you've done all you can. Just keep me informed if anything else happens. If you haven't heard from Chester Porter by the end of the day, I'll ring the emergency contact number he gave on his booking form.'

'Certainly, sir.'

David Rushworth had sounded very calm about it all. Perhaps she should take comfort from the fact that he hadn't held her to blame in any way. She could only hope he was still of the same mind if Chester failed to turn up at all.

By the time she arrived downstairs, at least half her party were already milling around in the entrance area.

Beryl and David Cox were the last to arrive.

'Sorry are we late? That's the trouble with long hair. It takes such an age to get dry.' Beryl's still damp hair was spread around her shoulders like a great cape.

'It's fine, you're not late.' Fiona lifted her guide pole and gathered everyone around her. 'I know we still have a couple of minutes in hand, but as you're all here, we might as well make a start. The forecast is good, and it looks as though we are in for a warm day, so we'll take it slowly. As he's tall, and everyone will be able to spot him easily, I've asked Greg if he will stay at the back to make sure we don't lose anybody so please don't get behind him when we pass through crowded areas. If we're all ready, follow me everyone and let's make our way to Donegal Square.'

The group emerged from their tour of the City Hall into glorious sunshine.

'That really was extraordinary. That great stairway was like a palace,' said Beryl Cox as they waited for the others to gather.

Once she had their attention, Fiona went into her spiel. 'I'd like us all to stand back a little so that we can see the whole of the front of the building. I'm sure you'll all appreciate how the sheer size and magnificent Renaissance-style architecture of the City Hall plus its sumptuous interior decoration demonstrate the great wealth of the city at the turn of the last century. Before we leave, let's take a closer look at the statue of Queen Victoria in front of us over to our right.'

Everyone moved a little closer.

'Do you see those two bronze statues on either side at its base? They represent the textile and shipbuilding industries which of course were the sources of that great wealth and growth of the city.'

Fiona waited until everyone had had time to take photos.

'We're going to move round to the left of the main building to see the Titanic Memorial and the Memorial Gardens.'

A few minutes later, as everyone gathered around another impressive statue, Fiona looked at Greg lingering at the corner waiting for the last of the photographers. He was clearly taking his role seriously. He had given no reaction when she'd told them that Chester still hadn't returned. Whether he was pleased the man had gone or feeling guilty that he had driven him away, there was no way of telling. Either way, she could only be grateful that he had stopped trying to give his version of events to any of others.

'Who is the main figure meant to be? A young Queen Victoria?' asked Irene Mullins.

'Actually no. That young lady is intended to represent disaster in the form of Death, or possibly Fate. She's holding a laurel wreath over the head of a drowned sailor lying at the base of the monument. And as you can see, he is being raised above the waves by a pair of mermaids.'

'It's beautiful,' said Irene almost to herself.

'Typical Victorian sentimentality, if you ask me.' Stephanie Jessen was clearly not so impressed.

'Perhaps the latest memorial is more to your taste.' Fiona turned and pointed to a long block of stone topped with engraved brass plates. 'That plinth and the small garden were opened on 15 April 2012, on the centenary of the disaster. This is the only memorial anywhere to commemorate all 1,512 victims of the Titanic – passengers and crew alike.'

Fiona stood back and watched as everyone trooped round to read some of the names inscribed on the long row of brass panels. This was obviously going to take some time. She couldn't help noticing Irene stealing a glance at Stephanie. The older woman was clearly upset by the younger woman's dismissive comment. Irene Mullins might like to chatter away and come out with the first thing that popped into her head, but she was a sensitive soul.

'Are we all ready to move on?'

As usual, Beryl quickly slid her way through to the front of the group. Not that anyone was likely to object. She would never see anything stuck at the back and she was short enough to be below everyone else's eyeline.

'Before we leave the area, I'm going to take you across the road to the Linen Hall Library which is the oldest library in Belfast. It was built in 1788 by the Belfast Society for the Promotion of Knowledge. It contains thousands of rare, old books known as the Irish book collection. We won't be going inside, but the reason I want to take you there is because, above the doorway, you'll see the Red Hand of Ulster which is the emblem of the Province.'

Despite its name, Donegall Square was more of a road that ran around the block of land on which the City Hall was built. Although it was no great distance, leading her party across the busy street was no easy task. Beryl managed to get separated in the throng of people crossing during one of the brief lulls in the traffic, but Colin spotted her and brought her back to the others. When they reached the library, Fiona did a quick head count. Greg gave her a thumbs-up sign. Between him and Colin, they were doing a good job.

'Can you all see the red hand on the plaque up there? Does anyone know why that red hand is the symbol of Ulster? Has anyone heard the story behind it?'

There was a great deal of head shaking.

'It stems from the legend about two Celtic heroes. They were racing across the sea to establish which one could touch the land of Ulster first. In his determination to win, one cut off his hand and threw it to the shore.'

'Gruesome!' Irene pulled a face and gave a little shiver. Those around her smiled, but not unkindly.

'We are now going to head south towards the Grand Opera House, but on the way, we are going to call in a rather nice café where we are going to have a well-deserved coffee stop.'

She had barely finished her sentence before a cheer went up.

'I could do with a sit-down for a bit,' said a smiling Norman Mullins.

Nine

Fiona had already phoned ahead to the small independent café to confirm the earlier reservation made by Head Office. Like many similar establishments in the area, the café was busy, which meant Fiona was all the more grateful for the company's foresight when she saw the reserved signs on the tables.

As everyone took their seats, she noticed Colin was still standing near the doorway, a dark frown on his normally smiling open countenance.

'Something wrong, Colin?'

He removed his glasses and waved them at her. 'It's these damned things. They're new. I only got them just before we came away. I thought I'd try a new look and went for these solid frames. Trouble is the blasted things are forever slipping down my nose. They're driving me mad. The assistant who did the fitting said that they might take a bit of getting used to after wearing glasses with nose pieces. What she didn't tell me was I'd be continually pushing the blasted things back up.'

'Oh dear.'

'It's no good. As soon as I get home I'm going to have to go and order my usual type. I wouldn't mind, but these stupid things were supposed to be designer spectacles and they cost me a bomb in the first place.'

Just about managing to keep a straight face, she said, 'I think we ought to go and join the others, don't you?'

Louise was already sitting down chatting with Stephanie

Jessen. Colin sat next to his wife and Fiona took the other empty chair.

'You're not still moaning about those glasses, are you?' Louise was fast losing patience.

Before the two could start sniping at each other, Fiona cut in, 'Thank you, Colin for helping Greg round up the back markers. It can be a bit of a nightmare even with small groups negotiating through the crowds in busy town centres. It's so easy to lose people.'

'I'm one of the culprits, I'm afraid,' admitted Stephanie. 'I prefer to take my photos when everyone's moved on so I can get a clear shot. Silly really. As soon as one group of people leave, another lot move in.'

Any fears that Fiona might have harboured after the earlier incident at Queen Victoria's statue that Stephanie might turn out to be an aloof young woman disdainful of her fellow passengers, were quickly dispelled. She turned out to be an amusing raconteur who was full of praise for everything she had seen to date.

'It's a much more attractive city than I ever imagined. I went for a stroll last night after dinner and ended up in a real Irish pub. It was terrific, with bands playing and everyone singing along. A really great atmosphere.'

'That was brave of you going into a bar on your own in a strange town,' said Fiona.

Stephanie shook her head vigorously, sending her flowing chestnut curls swinging. 'I didn't. I sat with David and Beryl at dinner last night and they invited me to join them. We had a fun evening. For such a tiny lady, Beryl has a fantastically powerful voice. She knew all the words, well most of them anyway. Belting them out with the best of them. Those two are a real laugh.'

'Sounds like you had a good time,' said Colin. He turned to his wife. 'Perhaps we should give the place a try tonight.'

'I can't remember what it was called. You'll have to ask the others. We just walked down the street until we found a pub with music and went in. I think Belfast is full of them.

You don't have to go far.'

'I don't know about its evening entertainment,' said Fiona, 'but one of the most famous Belfast pubs is the Crown Liquor Saloon which is not that far from here. It's a National Trust property. It claims to be the most photographed and filmed pub in the world.'

'Didn't I read somewhere that it was made famous as a film set for the classic James Mason film "Odd Man Out" back in the 1940s?' asked Colin, pushing his glasses further up his nose.

'That's right. But it does have a much older history. It was opened in 1876 as a workingmen's pub, but today it really is a showcase for the great Victorian craftsmanship of that era. The ceiling is magnificent, the windows are all stained glass, and mosaics cover the floors. Opposite the bar, there are separate little wooden snugs, which still have their original gas lamps. The carved wood side panels were originally made for the Britannic, which was the sister ship of the Titanic. The sheer detail throughout is quite breathtaking.'

'We've seen the pictures in our guidebook,' said Louise. 'It certainly looks worth a visit.'

'I'll point it out on our way to the theatre after we leave here,' said Fiona. 'We may only be a small group, but there are still too many of us to all pile in at once. We'll be able to take a quick peek in, but after we've been to the theatre and you all have some free time, those who want to have a proper look inside can do so and perhaps stop for a drink. It's marked on your city map in any case.'

As David Rushworth had pointed out, there was nothing she could practically do about her missing passenger, but that didn't stop her thoughts constantly returning to Chester Porter. By the time Fiona arrived back at the hotel, she felt surprisingly weary. She wondered if some of the older members of the group, such as Irene and Norman Mullins, might decide to opt out of the afternoon tour. The next oldest couple were Beryl and David Cox, but if Stephanie's comments about their antics last night were anything to go by, they were full of energy, so they were unlikely to want to miss out. Greg and Joan were probably in their early sixties and they were both fit and well.

As she walked down the open plan staircase into the main reception area, Rory was by the desk talking with another guest. As she reached the bottom step, he was there waiting for her.

'Any news?'

She shook her head. 'I take it that means the police haven't got back to the hotel either.'

'Sadly no. You have no idea what might have happened?'

Charming and caring though the hotel under-manager might be, he wasn't the person to whom she could divulge her secret fears. He didn't seem eager to get back to his duties and it was a few minutes before he returned to his duties.

By the time she arrived at the meeting point for the afternoon's tour near the main doors, Irene and Norman were sitting by the windows looking out over the comings and goings outside.

'You two have beaten me to it again.'

'Hello there, Fiona.' Irene's face lit up with a smile. 'We don't like being late. We were ready so we thought we might as well come down and wait here.'

'Have you had a nice morning?'

'Splendid, thank you, Fiona,' answered Norman.

'Did you take a look around the centre after the theatre?'

'We did think about popping into that National Trust pub you told us about, but decided as we're going to be on our feet again all afternoon we ought to pace ourselves and leave the pub for another day.'

'We were going to get a taxi back but there wasn't one around, so we started walking, didn't we, Norman. We passed this really nice little bakery and they had a tiny café section in the back, so we stopped for an early lunch and have one of their freshly prepared filled rolls.'

'And a naughty cake,' added her husband with a grin.

'We did share it,' Irene protested.

'It was good. The only thing was, I had trouble understanding what the waitress was saying. Her accent was so strong. I had to ask her three times to repeat herself.' Norman's face creased into a frown. 'It was embarrassing.'

'I'm having problems at times, but Norman's a bit deaf anyway and that makes it all the more difficult.'

Soon everyone was ready, and Fiona ushered them all onto the coach for the ten-minute drive for their Titanic Experience.

The sun was shining as they headed north on Queen's Road. It reflected off the great silver arms of the building with an almost blinding light.

'Some people say that the building looks like an iceberg, but each of those massive wings were designed to be the exact size and shape of the Titanic's hull. When we get to the entrance, I will get the tickets and then you can each take your time looking around the various exhibits. You'll each be given an audio guide. The coach will leave here at four thirty. If you would like to spend more time there and decide to walk back to the hotel or go and take a look at some of the other attractions in the Titanic Quarter, that won't be a problem. There's no need to let me know. If you are not on the coach at half-past four, we'll assume you're not coming.'

Ten

Fiona walked the length of the line of coaches in the car park for a second time, but there was no sign of the distinctive Super Sun coach. It wasn't like Winston to be late. He said he'd be back at four fifteen. She pulled her mobile out of her bag. Perhaps it would be best to make one last check to see if he'd left a message before making the call. He was probably on his way and she didn't like to ring him while he was driving, but at this rate she would have no choice. Wandering up and down by the coaches, she had no clear view of the approach road, so she made her way back to the car park entrance.

She let out a great sigh of relief when she saw the white coach with its yellow stripe driving towards her.

As soon as he'd backed into a space between two monster coaches, she hurried to the door waiting for him to open it.

'I was getting worried for a moment there, Winston.' She tried to make her voice light and jokey, but she wasn't sure she'd succeeded.

'Sorry, sweetheart. Bit of a problem with the traffic. I've had to drive halfway around the city to get here.'

'Oh?'

'The police have cordoned off some of the streets in the centre and the traffic's piled up all over the place.'

'Do you know why?'

'When we were stuck in the traffic, I asked a taxi driver if he knew what the holdup was and he said he'd heard over his radio from another driver that there'd been some sort of incident outside one of the hospitals.'

'An accident?'

'He thought it was a shooting.'

'My goodness me.'

Before she could ask anything more, the first passengers were already at the bottom of the coach steps. Time for action.

'I'll go back and direct the rest to the coach as they arrive.' Fiona skipped down the steps and helped Irene and Norman on board before heading to the car park entrance.

It wasn't long before she spotted Greg and Joan Fletcher walking towards her talking earnestly. Joan looked up and noticed Fiona. She almost ran the closing distance.

'Fiona! Did you know? Someone's been shot in the middle of Belfast. Greg was just checking his phone while he was waiting for me in the shop just now.'

Any hope of getting back to the hotel without her passengers knowing were now dashed. They would all find out sometime of course, but this kind of drip feed of information always caused more panic than was warranted when the full story came out.

Once she had rounded up the last of her party and returned to the coach, everyone seemed to be talking at once.

'Do you think it's one of those dreadful ISIS attacks?' Irene asked.

'I very much doubt it,' Fiona attempted to reassure the clearly distressed woman. 'As far as I know, Muslim terrorists don't have any major arguments with the Irish.'

'It could be part of this sectarian thing. I read somewhere that it's been flaring up again in recent months,' David's drawn-out Northumberland voice was clearly heard from the back of the coach.

'Let's wait until we can find out more before we jump to any conclusions. I'm going to assume that those who are not here are planning to make their own way back so please settle down and fasten your seatbelts and we can go.'

Fiona had no wish to spend the next couple of hours before dinner cooped up in her room. It was such a beautiful day it would be a shame to waste the opportunity for a gentle walk along the riverside. She could find somewhere to sit outside in the sun rather than having tea in the hotel café.

It proved a little more difficult to find somewhere suitable than she had anticipated, but she eventually found a small café with an outside table on a side street. Even without facing onto the attractive riverside, it was pleasant sitting idly watching the world go by. Hectic confusion might be taking place only a few streets away in the city centre, but here relative peace and quiet was the order of the day. She closed her eyes and lifted her face to the sun.

Eventually, pulling herself back to the present, she glanced at her watch and decided that if she was going to leave herself time for a leisurely shower before dinner, it was time to pay her bill and make tracks for the hotel.

On the way back, she came across a group of life-sized bronze sculptures of a shepherd herding half a dozen sheep. Quite what that had to do with the centre of Belfast she had no idea, but they were definitely worth a photo or two.

She was crouched down on one knee trying to get a long shot to include the whole flock when she heard footsteps approaching.

'Need a hoist up?'

She took Douglas Redhill's proffered hand and pulled herself back onto her feet brushing the dust from the leg of her trousers.

'Thanks, Douglas.'

The two of them walked back together.

'Did you enjoy the Titanic Experience this afternoon?'

He nodded. 'The audio guide was quite good.'

They chatted for a few minutes before Fiona asked, 'What made you choose this tour? Is this your first visit to Belfast?'

'I have been before, but only for work, so I didn't get a chance to see much of the sights. It's a great place.'

This seemed as good a time as any for her to ask him about Chester.

'We don't often get single men of your age on our tours, and this time I have two of you. Or rather, had.'

'Still no word on Chester?'

'No. It's very strange. I must confess, I didn't really get to know him. I think we only had a couple of conversations before he went missing.'

'Me neither.'

'Really? I wondered, you two both being on your own and roughly the same age, if you might have spent a bit more time together.'

'A group of us ended up in the same pub that first evening we were here, but we were all just watching the chap playing the fiddle and listening to the music.' He laughed. 'It was a bit noisy in there for general conversation.'

'I can imagine.'

'He left before me and I don't think we said more than half a dozen words to each other all evening.'

By now, they had arrived at the main doors of the hotel. Douglas stood back and let her go in front of him.

It was hardly surprising that the shooting was the main topic of conversation at dinner that evening. Even before her party entered the Sonoma Restaurant, Fiona found several of them clustered outside the doors sharing the snippets of information they had discovered.

'I heard the man who got shot was visiting his mother in hospital.'

'But I thought he was supposed to be a terrorist,' said Irene, her face puckering in a worried frown. Neither she nor her husband had caught up with the digital age and clearly felt at a disadvantage when those around them appeared to be in the know by accessing the latest news on their smartphones or iPads. 'Is that how the police managed to track him down?'

'It wasn't the police who shot him. He was already in

police custody,' explained Louise.

Several people started talking at once. All with a slightly different angle on the story.

Colin pulled his smartphone out of his pocket and tapped the news app to show her. 'It says here that the victim was Eamon McCollum, a known CIRA activist…'

'I thought that was something to do with America,' muttered Norman.

'CIRA stands for Continuity Irish Republican Army,' Louise explained. 'They're a group of republicans who refused to give up the fight for independence from Britain after the IRA was disbanded following the signing of the Peace Agreement. That's what it said on the BBC news.'

'Anyway,' Colin continued reading, 'McCollum was on remand after guns and bomb-making equipment were found in his lockup two weeks ago. He was shot in the chest as he left the Royal Victoria's Critical Care Unit where he was being taken to visit his dying mother. The prison officer to whom he was handcuffed, also received a bullet wound to the upper arm. McCollum died shortly after the incident. The officer is still receiving treatment.'

'Does it say if the police managed to catch the killer?' Fiona asked.

Colin shook his head. 'Apparently not. The shooter was a pillion passenger on a motorbike. Both riders were dressed in black leathers with full helmets so totally unrecognisable. The police attempted to give chase, but the bike headed north on Lisburn Road before turning off the wrong way down a one-way street weaving between the oncoming traffic. There was no way the police cars could follow. Large sections of the city centre still remain closed.'

'That much we do know,' David Cox said with feeling. 'It took us so long to drive back from the Titanic exhibition this afternoon, we could have walked it quicker.'

Seizing the temporary lull in the chatter, Fiona said firmly, 'Perhaps we should go in, everyone. We are holding up other hotel guests.'

Day 5 Thursday

Once we leave our hotel, the coach will head out of Belfast on the motorway, then inland driving north through Ballymena and the village of Ballymoney and on to the Giant's Causeway on the north coast of County Antrim.

Often described as the eighth wonder of the world, the Giant's Causeway was designated a Unesco World Heritage site in 1986, the only designated site in Northern Ireland. It was declared a national nature reserve in 1987 by the Department of the Environment for Northern Ireland.

The causeway is an area of about 40,000 interlocking basalt columns formed 60 million years ago when a thick layer of molten basaltic lava flowed along an existing valley of chalk beds. It extends along the coast for four miles.

The tops of the columns form steppingstones that stretch from the foot of the cliff to disappear under the sea. Most of the columns are hexagonal, although there are also some with four, five, seven or eight sides. The tallest are almost 40 feet high, and the solidified lava in the cliffs is 92 feet thick in places.

Our coach will drop us at the new visitor centre which was opened in 2012. The modern design of the building was inspired by the natural columns of the Giant's Causeway and it has a sloping grass roof.
In the centre, you'll find touch-screens to help you learn more about the formation of the Causeway and you'll hear the legend of the Irish giant Finn McCool.

Lunch will be at a nearby hotel before we make the short journey to the Old Bushmills Distillery. The distillery prides itself on being the world's oldest. We will see the display of old equipment in the small museum and have a tour of the distillery, which will end with a tasting session in the 1608 bar in the former malt kilns.

Before heading back to Belfast, we will take a short diversion along the coast road to see the rope bridge at Carrick-a-Rede. Suspended almost 100 feet above the sea, it was first erected by salmon fishermen in 1755.

We will continue along the coast road to the resort town of Ballycastle, famous for its traditional horse fair. Near the sea front, we will pass the memorial to

Marconi who, in 1898, sent the first wireless message from here to Rathlin Island some eight miles off the coast.
Super Sun Executive Travel

Eleven

'Do you think we'll have any problems getting out of the city this morning?'

Winston shook his head. 'I shouldn't think so, sweetheart. I expect they'll have removed all the roadblocks by now, and in any case, we'll be heading north not back into the centre. It shouldn't make any difference to our timings.'

'Does that mean we can still expect to be at the Giant's Causeway by ten-thirty?'

'No problem.'

'It won't really matter if we are not exactly on time in any case. The only crucial timings are at the hotel for lunch and at Bushmills for our distillery tour immediately after. We've got timed tickets for the full tasting experience.' She leant forward, elbows on the table, chin in her hands, looking at her driver with an impish grin. 'You know, Winston, the number of whiskey, wine and beer tastings we seem to do, I often think we ought to rename Super Sun Tours, the Boozy Tours.'

He gave one of his deep rumbling laughs. 'The passengers always seem to enjoy 'em.'

'True, but once you've been round one distillery, winery or brewery, it all gets a bit the same. As far as I'm concerned, they are the least interesting part of the tour.'

Winston chuckled. 'That's 'cause you're teetotal, sweetheart.'

Fiona pulled a face. 'Not quite. I might not drink on tour, but I do have the occasional glass of wine at home.

Christmas and special occasions.'

He gave an indulgent grin which she ignored. She picked up her spoon and half-heartedly chased an elusive piece of melon around the plate. 'I wasn't planning on giving everyone too much general information on the way up. I don't think I could possibly talk solidly for an hour and half anyway. But I might start with some general patter a little earlier than I'd planned just to stop them fussing over yesterday's shooting. I know once the talk of the victim being a known terrorist hit the headlines, the Mullinses were worried about reprisal attacks and I think several of the others are a little anxious about what might happen too.'

'Perhaps it's a good thing that we'll be out of Belfast all day then. Come to think of it, we'll be heading out of the city for the next couple of days after that, so that can't be bad now, can it?'

She gave him a weak smile. 'That's true. And even on Saturday, we'll be visiting Mount Stewart House and Strangford Lough for most of the day. Let's keep our fingers crossed that by then, things will have settled down. If not, we may have to organise a last-minute trip somewhere away from Belfast instead of the scheduled free time in the city first thing.'

'You just enjoy your breakfast, sweetheart. No point giving yourself indigestion. Not much we can do about it so let's just wait and see. We'll cope. We always do.'

Fiona gave a little chuckle and picked up her teacup. 'You know there are times when I'm convinced that I must have an anti-stress button that you, Winston Taylor, are the only person who knows how to press.'

'That's what I'm here for, sweetheart.'

A very dishevelled-looking Andrew Salmon walked into Montgomery-Jones's office and slumped into an easy chair.

'Coffee?'

'I'd prefer something stronger.' From the look on Salmon's face, he was only half-joking.

Montgomery-Jones picked up the phone and requested coffee. He put a hand over the mouthpiece and turned to Salmon, 'When was the last time you ate something?'

Salmon shrugged his shoulders.

Montgomery-Jones finished the call and walked over to take the easy chair opposite Salmon. 'I take it you have been working through the night?'

'Not quite. I grabbed a couple of hours' sleep, but it's been non-stop at Thames House since the news broke. I'm off home now for a quick shower and a change of clothes.' He ran a hand through his hair brushing it back from his forehead.

'I take it you are no closer to finding your gunman?'

Salmon shook his head and lay back in the chair rubbing his eyes. 'The trouble is we've no real idea who he and his accomplices might be. The Press are all asking if this is the restart of the Troubles. It's pure speculation of course. There is no evidence to suggest it's anything to do with any of the loyalist paramilitary groups. The Orange Volunteer Force have been very active lately, but it's not their style not to claim responsibility. That's the whole point, let the other side know that they can play hardball. They want the publicity. And that goes for any of the other Ulster loyalist groups too.'

They were interrupted by a gentle knock at the door. A tray of coffee was laid on the small table set between the two easy chairs. 'We've sent out for a couple of bacon rolls for you, sir,' the smartly dressed middle-aged woman said to Salmon. 'I'll bring them in as soon as they arrive.'

'Thank you.'

'Would you like me to pour for you, sir?' She looked at Montgomery-Jones.

'I will see to it. Thank you, Alice.'

When the door closed, Salmon continued, 'I wouldn't be surprised if it wasn't one of his own group. According to my informant, there's a lot of dissent in the inner circle. It seems there are internal rumblings from those who claim all the recent failures are because McCollum was getting careless and that the man had had his day. Thanks to our undercover man, we've been able to foil several shipments of arms coming in and thwarted a planned attack on a major target. Anyway, the diehards in the group, who fought in the Troubles, are worried about a takeover by the up-and-coming new bloods jockeying to take over. These younger ones in their twenties and early thirties are demanding more action. They're not happy with the softly-softly approach they claim McCollum and his old guard are taking. There's a lot of suspicion and finger-pointing going on.'

Montgomery-Jones poured the coffee and placed a cup on the table in front of Salmon.

'Thanks.' Salmon picked it up and took a sip before continuing. 'The point is we need to find these culprits fast. The longer all this goes on, the more likely the talk of turf wars between republicans and loyalists will escalate into a reality. You and I both know that the so-called peace in Northern Ireland is held together with sticky tape. If we can prove McCollum was the victim of a revenge killing by someone unrelated to the political scene or even one of his own inner circle, we might just be able to stick on another layer of Sellotape.'

'I presume the CCTV footage was no help?'

'Dead end. The bike was followed along the main road weaving through traffic, up onto the pavements and turning down a couple of side streets. It disappeared down a narrow pedestrian path into an area without any cameras and was never picked up again.'

'False number plates, I presume.'

'Naturally. The bike was a Norton Dominator, a common enough make and model, and the two riders must have hidden it away somewhere together with their biking gear because there is no bike on cameras in that part of the city within a suitable time frame.'

'I take it the details of McCollum's visit to the hospital were not public knowledge?'

Salmon shook his head. 'I would imagine there's quite a furore with the prison service blaming the police and vice versa for the leak. I suppose the source could even have been one of the hospital staff.'

Montgomery-Jones said, 'Apart from the inside information about the visit, the gunman would need to know the exact time McCollum was due to leave the building. I take it the missing brother of the witness you mentioned on your previous visit is no longer on your suspect list? The attack was clearly not the work of a single individual. Apart from his fellow rider, the gunman presumably had help disposing of the bike.'

'True, but we still can't trace Masterson and he is the only person who's made such a public threat. We do know he emptied his bank account the morning he disappeared. At this stage, we're not prepared to rule him out, however unlikely. The thing is, there is a rumour that when Masterson made this big thing on Twitter about getting even with McCollum some time ago, this small newish outfit calling themselves the Ulster Action Group who also have a personal axe to grind with McCollum and his cell, made contact with him.'

'Meaning there is a possibility that they are the ones providing the backup Masterson needed?'

'Let's just say we can't ignore the idea.'

There was another knock at the door.

'Your rolls have arrived.' Montgomery-Jones got to his feet, went to the door and took the proffered plate.

For a couple of minutes, there was silence while Salmon greedily tucked into his late breakfast. When he'd finished, he wiped his lips and fingers with the paper napkin, scrunched it up and dropped it onto the plate with a satisfied sigh.

'I didn't realise how hungry I was until I started eating. Anyway, to get back to why I'm here. Obviously, the Belfast Police are keeping us informed of everything that might have even the slightest bearing on the case. I know Chief

Superintendent Dailey personally, and – this may have absolutely nothing to do with the case – according to him a passenger on a coach tour has gone missing. It was a couple of days ago, but he hasn't been seen since. No one made any connection at first, but I asked Dailey to let me know if anything at all occurred that was out of the ordinary. He got in touch first thing this morning. One of my people followed up on the details, which is really why I'm here.'

'Oh?'

'The coach company concerned is Super Sun.'

For a brief moment, silence hung in the air. 'And you are going to tell me that the tour manager is a certain Mrs Fiona Mason.'

Salmon gave a wry laugh. 'After what happened in Brussels last summer, it does seem an amazing coincidence. Of course, as I said, the odds that it has anything remotely connected to McCollum are a hundred to one, but I thought you'd want to know.'

'I presume you are investigating the missing man's background?'

Salmon nodded. 'As the information has only just come through, we haven't got very far, but there was no answer to the man's home telephone number and the emergency contact number he gave the coach company is a mobile number which is invalid. That's why Dailey thought I might be interested. The false emergency number could be a genuine mistake of course. It happens surprisingly frequently apparently. Filling in forms, people often transpose numbers. Doing it online, it's easy to mistype and the possibility of staff error when transferring data from handwritten forms doubles the problem.'

Salmon glanced across at Montgomery-Jones who was now leaning back in the chair with his long legs stretched out in front of him, his elbows resting on the arms of the chair steepling his fingers, obviously deep in thought.

'The contact name alone is not much use to us,' Salmon continued. 'We have no way of knowing if it's a relative or a friend and the mobile number gives us no idea of his location. He could be living in any part of the country. We are still waiting on the verification of the resident at the missing man's given address. One of his neighbours might be able to shed some light on the matter. We'll have to see. He's roughly the same height and build as Masterson, but with no photograph of the passenger, not even a passport photograph, that may also prove inconclusive.'

'But you must have a photograph of Masterson. Surely you have sent a copy to Mrs Mason for comparison purposes?'

Salmon hunched his shoulders and sank lower into the chair. 'Not a lot of point,' he said defensively. 'All the pictures we have of Masterson show him with a beard and glasses. We know from the initial description of the missing passenger that he was clean-shaven and there was no mention of spectacles. Contact lenses and a quick shave and the man would be virtually unrecognisable without expert digital comparison. It's still early days of course. We've only just got the information, but I thought you might want to know as soon as possible.'

Now it was Montgomery-Jones's turn to put his hands to his face and wipe across his eyelids with the tips of his fingers.

Twelve

They drove through the market town of Ballymena heading north towards the village of Ballymoney. Fiona picked up the microphone.

'You may have noticed that several towns begin with "Bally" such as Ballycastle and Ballyvoy which we'll see this afternoon and there's a Ballygally on the coast road that we'll pass through later in the week. Bally is the Celtic word for town or more accurately, townland.'

She spent the next few minutes telling them more about the Giant's Causeway and describing its formation.

Irene in the seat behind Fiona pulled a face. 'I understand that lava cooled but why did it form into hexagonal blocks? You don't see that in other places. Our daughter showed us her holiday pictures of Iceland and the lava was nothing like that.'

'It does depend on the type of lava. You've seen how the mud cracks into little blocks when puddles dry out?' The older woman nodded. 'Well the same thing happened to the basalt lava in this region as it cooled and solidified from top to bottom, contracting to form regular shapes. Then erosion gradually cut down into the lava flow and the basalt split along those cracks to form the hexagonal columns. When we get to the information centre, I'm sure you'll find plenty of diagrams and short videos that will explain it much better than I can.'

It may be one of the smallest groups that Fiona had been asked to lead, but as she was discovering, they certainly liked to keep her on her toes with questions. She made a mental note to spend some time this evening thoroughly reading her notes and checking the internet for the following day's tour.

'Of course, there is another theory altogether. That it was built by the great Irish giant, Finn McCool. Finn decided to build the causeway from the North coast of Antrim across to the Scottish island of Staffa so that he could confront his enemy the Scottish giant, Brenandonner. Finn was so tired when he'd finished that he lay down and went to sleep. He was woken by the thunderous sound of Brenandonner's footsteps. He realised that Brenandonner must be at least twice his size, so he leapt to his feet and raced back home. Finn's wife dressed him in baby clothes and made him lie in a makeshift cradle. When Brenandonner reached Finn's house, Finn's wife told him to hush or he'd wake the baby. Seeing the size of the so-called baby, Brenandonner decided he was no match for a huge giant that must be almost twice his size, so he ran back to Scotland ripping up the causeway as he retreated. All that remains today are the two ends – the Giant's causeway in Ireland and similar formations at Fingal's Cave on the island of Staffa. I'll leave you to hear more about that story when we get to the centre. They have an excellent big screen cartoon film with the story in full.'

'I think I like that theory much better than the one about mud puddles,' laughed Irene.

Once they arrived at the visitor centre, Fiona went to buy the tickets. She made sure that everyone had picked up an audio guide and checked they each knew how it worked. Now she could leave her passengers to their own devices for a couple of hours.

It was no surprise, given that it was July and peak season, that the visitor centre was crowded so Fiona decided to visit the causeway first and leave the centre until later. She had already decided to walk down the steep winding path, but outside, one look at the length of the queue waiting for the shuttle bus was enough to convince her that she had made the correct decision.

She had only gone a few hundred yards, when her mobile began to ring.

'Is this a good time?'

'Mr Rushworth! Yes, certainly.'

'Good. I checked your itinerary and hoped you'd be free. I won't keep you, but I was a bit concerned how things were going after what happened yesterday. Has that dreadful shooting caused any problems?'

'No, sir. We did have to take a few detours, and our journey back from the Titanic Belfast took three times longer than expected, but today we had no holdups leaving the city.'

'I was thinking more about the effect it might have had on your passengers.'

'It has tended to dominate the conversation,' she replied lightly, 'but no one's expressed any major concern about their own safety or demanded to return to Britain, if that's what you mean. I did advise them that it might not be a sensible idea to go into the city centre last night after dinner, which I know some of them were planning earlier in the day. The hotel has a very pleasant lounge bar and I think most people were happy to sit there enjoying the lovely views. The riverside is attractive all lit up at night.'

'That is good news. If anyone does change their mind and start making a fuss, the company is quite happy to fly them back at our expense. Obviously, don't suggest it, but if anyone does approach you, you have my authority to give them that option.'

'I'll bear that in mind. Thank you, sir.'

'Before you go there is one more thing. No more news about your missing passenger, I take it?'

'I'm afraid not, sir. I'm not sure that we can expect the police to do very much about finding him. He is an adult and doesn't come into any vulnerable category, plus after yesterday's incident, I would think they have a lot to deal with right now.'

'I do know they are not ignoring it. I had a phone call early this morning asking for details about him. I had to tell them that all we have is his address and travel insurance details. I don't suppose you have any information that might help?'

'Such as?'

'Anything to do with his background that he might have talked about. Family or even which company he works for.'

'To be honest, I've only spoken to him a couple of times and then only in passing.'

'I expect the police will be in touch with you again sometime. Let me know what they say. Anyway, enjoy the rest of your trip.'

'Thank you, sir.'

Fiona slipped her mobile back into her bag. The Tours Director had sounded strangely on edge. David Rushworth had always struck her as a confident, unflappable individual. Was there something she was not being told?

One of the features on the causeway that Fiona had told her passengers to look out for was a large rock shaped like a giant's boot. It wasn't difficult to find, lying just off the main path not far from the start of the trail. She saw a rather grim-looking Colin Davenport standing staring at the group of teenagers taking turns to climb up and sit on top to have their photos taken by the others on their mobile phones.

'Waiting to take a photo, Colin?' Fiona asked when she reached him.

'Ten minutes those kids have been larking around. Louise got tired of waiting for me. She disappeared ages ago.'

Fiona stayed talking with Colin for a couple of minutes when the teenagers suddenly decided they'd had enough and began to move off. As the last one bent to pick up his rucksack lying at the foot of the rock, three Japanese tourists suddenly appeared and before Colin could raise his camera, walked in front of him heading for the rock.

Fiona decided it was best to beat a tactful retreat and

walked further along the path towards the Shepherd's Steps.

Fiona had allowed herself plenty of time to get back to the visitor centre to look around before her passengers began to gather to go back to the coach. She even had time to wander around the shop, not that she was interested in buying anything.

She looked at the various books on offer and turned to see Stephanie Jessen inspecting the selection of long multi-coloured scarves hanging on a rail in the clothing section.

'Hi, Stephanie. Not buying another scarf?' Fiona said in mock surprise. Every day the young woman appeared wearing a different scarf wound around her throat.

Stephanie turned and smiled. 'I'm not really one for jewellery, but I will admit to having a weakness for pretty scarves. Now which do you think? The greeny-blue one or the pink and purple?' She held up the two hangers, gently wafting them to and fro to see how the fabric shimmered in the changing light.

'Definitely the green one. It goes so well with those lustrous chestnut waves of yours.'

Ignoring Fiona's compliment, Stephanie said, 'Green it is then.'

Stephanie hung the other back on the rail and Fiona walked with her to the till.

'Did you enjoy the causeway?'

'Yes, thank you, Fiona.'

'Did you walk to the end?'

'Just about.'

'Well done you,' said Fiona with a smile. 'I saw the Organ which I thought was pretty impressive, but I confess I never made it as far as the Amphitheatre.'

'I'm not sure you really missed much. It wasn't that different from the previous sections. To tell you the truth, I found the whole thing a bit of a disappointment. After all those splendid photographs you see on the internet and in books, it was much smaller than I imagined it would be.'

'It does continue along the coast for quite some way, but that far section has been closed for a few years now. I don't suppose it helps having all those people crowding over it everywhere.'

Stephanie was clearly not in the best of moods. Perhaps this was not such a good time to broach the subject Fiona had come over to ask in the first place, but she might not get another chance.

'I've been meaning to ask you, Stephanie. You were talking to Chester Porter…'

'What are you trying to say? That I had something to do with his disappearance?' Stephanie spun on her heel and glared at Fiona.'

'Not at all!' Fiona took a step back. 'What I meant was, you were sitting with him and Louise and Colin Davenport at breakfast on that first morning. I just wondered if he had mentioned anything about his family, where he worked or what kind of job he did. These things often tend to come up when you chat with people on holiday. The police want to know as much as they can about him in the hope that it will help them find him. I'm asking everyone in the group.'

'Oh, I see. Sorry, didn't mean to jump down your throat.' She shook her head. 'I can't think of anything off hand.'

'Never mind, it was only a long shot.'

Fiona was about to hurry away when Stephanie called her back. 'Wait a sec. There was one thing. I think he said he came from somewhere on the Wirral.'

'Thank you, Stephanie.'

Chester Porter's address was the one thing they did have. The address he gave was in Ashton-under-Lyne a few miles east of Manchester. Stephanie was obviously mixing up Chester with Douglas Redhill; although technically, Ellesmere Port was just south of the Wirral. Fiona made her way to the cloakrooms. It would soon be time to start gathering everyone up and there would be the inevitable queue for the women's toilets. There always was.

Thirteen

Lunch had been arranged in a hotel a little further along the coast from the information centre. The hotel had set aside two tables of six. Fiona contemplated sitting with the Davenports so she could ask them if they remembered Chester saying anything about his background. She had planned to ask Colin earlier during their brief encounter on the causeway by the Giant's Boot but had rejected it straight away. The mood Colin was in at the time was not conducive to seemingly general banter. In the event, one table was already full with the two remaining unaccompanied passengers and two of the other couples including the Davenports so no chance to chat with either of them over lunch. Still, she had shared a table with them several times already so perhaps it was not such a bad idea to get to know some of her other passengers. If only she could remember who was sitting with Chester at dinner on the first evening. Meals were probably the most likely time for such things to crop up in general conversation especially at the beginning of the tour.

Fiona took a seat between Joan Fletcher and David Cox. Not surprisingly, the main topic of conversation was about their experiences of the morning.

As they all tucked into their steak and Guinness pie, Fiona asked, 'Did anyone go right up to the top?'

'You mean up the Shepherd's Steps?' asked Joan. 'It was bad enough walking half-way up the hillside on the lower path. It was quite windy.'

It seemed no one at the table had ventured that far. David and Beryl hadn't bothered to go further than the first section, but they all seemed to have enjoyed the visit.

It was Beryl who brought up the subject of their missing fellow passenger. 'Has there been any more news about Chester, Fiona? He seemed such a nice man. Do you think something's happened to him? Have you checked the hospitals?'

Fiona nodded. 'It was the first thing we did. I do know the police are still looking.'

'Do people often go missing on your tours, pet?' joked David Cox, lightening the mood.

'Thankfully not!' It wasn't exactly a lie; he had qualified the question with the word "often". Nonetheless, Fiona had no intention of telling them about the man who went missing in Keukenhof Gardens on her very first tour. Especially as his body was found a few days later stuffed into a large rubbish skip behind a deserted café. She could only pray that the same thing wasn't going to happen again this time and that Chester would soon reappear unharmed.

'I don't think I got to speak to him that much,' said David. 'We said hello at the cocktail party in Liverpool, but that was about it.'

'He was on our table that first evening at dinner. He sat opposite; don't you remember?' prompted his wife.

David frowned. 'Not really.'

'Well, I have to admit, he wasn't much of a talker,' said Beryl.

'I'm surprised the poor man managed to get a word in edgeways, the way you natter away half the time, pet,' David said with a laugh, pushing away his empty plate.

'Oh, you!' Beryl gave her husband an affectionate punch on his arm.

'Did he mention if he had any family at all?' asked Fiona.

'David asked him what line of work he was in and they started talking about semiconductors.' She turned to her husband, 'Don't you remember?'

David frowned. 'Vaguely.'

'All above my head, I'm afraid. Complete technophobe me. I have enough problems trying to work out how to switch on these new-fangled smart phones, tablets and digital recorders without trying to understand how they work,' his wife muttered with feeling.

'Did Chester happen to mention which company he worked for by any chance?'

David scratched his chin. 'Not that I recall.'

If anyone considered her question strange, no one showed it. Not that Fiona could see why the police were so keen to know about Chester's background. Surely, there were all sorts of electoral rolls and other records they had easy access to if they wanted to know more about him.

Unless he was attending a meeting in another building, an increasing occurrence these days, Montgomery-Jones rarely left Vauxhall Cross for lunch. Today he felt in need of a breath of fresh air, in as much as air in the busy streets of central London could be said to be fresh. It was a warm, sunny day, but there was a pleasant breeze from the river as he walked along the Albert Embankment up towards Lambeth Palace.

More by chance than design, he decided to stop at "The Rose". He had eaten at the traditional Victorian public house several times before and always found the food acceptable. The main attraction today was that he could sit outside and enjoy the views of the Houses of Parliament on the far side of the Thames as he ate.

He took a seat at the only vacant table and looked at the menu. A short, rather plump girl in her late teens with spiky pink hair emerged from inside with two plates of roast lamb and aubergine which she laid in front of the couple at the next table. The smell of the Welsh lamb was tempting, but a large lunch was not conducive to an afternoon of clear thought.

'I will have a smoked salmon blini and an espresso,

please,' he said to the girl with the startling hairdo when she arrived at his table.

He was in no great hurry. One of the reasons he had decided to leave his office was because he wanted to mull over what Andrew Salmon had told him earlier. He could do that better away from the constant interruption of phone calls.

The possibility that Fiona Mason's missing passenger had anything to do with the disappearance of Edward Masterson was so remote as to be hardly worth considering. The reason that it was of any interest at all was that at least so far, it was proving difficult to find any background on Fiona's missing passenger. The fact that it was still on his mind at all was no doubt because the man was one of her passengers. The woman had an almost magical ability to infiltrate herself into his affairs.

'Someone looks happy.'

He turned sharply and looked up at the waitress. 'I beg your pardon?'

She grinned at him. 'Sorry, sir. Didn't mean to make you jump. It's just that you had this big smile on your face and a kind of dreamy look in your eye.'

She placed his coffee on the table in front of him and said quickly. 'Your blini won't be much longer.'

She disappeared before he could reply.

After he'd eaten, Montgomery-Jones pushed away his plate and contemplated whether to order a second cup of coffee. He was about to signal the waitress when his mobile started beeping. He glanced at the name of the caller and raised an eyebrow.

'Salmon. This is a surprise. Has there been a development?'

'You could say that. Sorry to ring you on your mobile. I did try your office, but they said you were out, and I thought you'd want to know straightaway. I've just had a call from Chief Superintendent Dailey. They've found a body.

Fourteen

'Our original grant to distil whiskey was signed in 1608 by King James I, making Bushmills Ireland's oldest distillery. There has been distillation on this site ever since, using the unique water from our own stream and local Irish barley. The word whiskey comes from a Gaelic word that means "the water of life". The process of distillation was brought to Ireland by monks from Asia over a thousand years ago. Small scale production became part of the Irish way of life, but in the 17th century, the English introduced a licensing system and started to close down the local stills.'

As their guide continued to drone on relating the history of whiskey production, Fiona noticed Norman muttering to his wife. When the guide had finished his spiel, and the group moved on to the next section, Fiona eased her way through to his side.

'Is there a problem, Norman?'

'No, no.'

Fiona was not so sure. 'Is it the accent again? Our guide is quite difficult to tune in to.'

'Exactly. But it's nothing to worry about.'

'I didn't understand much of that last bit either,' admitted Irene. 'About why it all declined.'

'He was explaining how the demand dropped because of the poverty caused by the potato famine and then the Temperance movement didn't help, so Northern Ireland lost its exports to the growing Scottish whisky producers.'

'I thought he said things were improving recently.'

'Yes, he did.'

'I'm not really a whiskey man, but I do love the odd Irish coffee after a posh meal out and you like your Bailey's at Christmas, don't you love?'

The three of them caught up with the group in time to hear their guide assure them all with a great sense of pride, that Irish whiskey was considerably better than its Scottish counterpart because it was triple distilled to give it its smoothness and richness as opposed to Scotch which went through the distillation process only twice.

At the end of the tour of the distillery, they were all shepherded into the tasting room.

'This is the best bit,' said David Cox rubbing his hands with glee at the sight of the tables laid out with green place mats labeled with the various varieties thus indicating they were about to sample several different whiskeys. David's was not the only face wreathed in smiles at the prospect.

As the group were ushered to a set of tables and invited to sit down, Fiona stood to the side and watched.

It wasn't long before Irene came to join her.

'Are you not drinking?' Fiona asked.

'I had a sip of the first one, but…' She wrinkled her nose and pulled a face.

'I think they have some soft drinks if that's what you'd prefer.'

Irene shook her head. 'I'm fine, dear. Are you not a drinker or are you not allowed to drink on duty as it were?'

'The company doesn't have any rules about tour managers not drinking, but I'm not really much of a drinker even back home.'

As they settled themselves on the high stools by the bar area, Irene said, 'That empty chair at our table reminded me of poor Chester. I remember him saying how he was going to buy a bottle of special whiskey here in the shop. Apparently, they only sell it here so he can't get it back home.'

It had never occurred to Fiona that Irene might have

learnt something of Chester's background. He had gone missing so early, she'd thought that few of the other passengers would have had much of an opportunity to talk with him at any length. She should have realised that the motherly, talkative Irene was an obvious candidate.

'I have to confess, I really didn't get a chance to chat to Mr Porter,' Fiona said. 'Does that mean he's been here before, do you know?'

'To the distillery?' Irene looked thoughtful. 'I don't think so. He wanted it as a present. Something a bit special for a friend he said.'

'I see.' So Chester hadn't lied when he said he'd never been to Northern Ireland before.

'He seemed such a pleasant young man. I do hope he's all right. We talked quite a bit about Australia. Our daughter, Angela and her family live out there and so does his sister apparently. It's such a small world, isn't it?'

'Hmm.' Fiona gave her an encouraging smile.

'I asked him if he'd been out to visit her, especially as she's his only relation. He said she's a lot older than him and they've sort of lost touch. They exchange Christmas cards, as you do, but that's about it. I said that was a great shame and he should make the effort to get back in contact. He said it was funny I should say that because he was thinking about doing just that these last few weeks. He was hoping to go out there to see her. Trouble is, Australia is such a long way to go and you really need to spend a month or two there to make the journey worthwhile, and he couldn't take that much time off work at the moment. That was one of the reasons he chose to come on this trip, because it was only a week. He was going to negotiate with his company about carrying over the rest of this year's holiday allocation so he could go out there next Spring.'

'Did he happen to mention which company he worked for?'

Irene wrinkled her face in concentration. 'If he did, I don't remember. I know his job was very technical, something that I didn't really understand.'

If Irene thought it odd that Fiona was asking such questions, she didn't show it. It might not be much, but at least when she got back to the hotel, she had something to pass on to the police. Quite how that might help to find the man, Fiona couldn't fathom, but hers was not to reason why.

Their next stop was on the coast at the famous Carrick-a-Rede Rope Bridge near Ballintoy, which connected the mainland and Carrick-a-Rede Island. Although the sun was shining, the 66-foot bridge of narrow planks with rope handrails spanning the deep chasm below was swaying in the strong wind.

'Are we going across?' Colin Davenport looked excited at the prospect.

'I'm afraid not,' Fiona said quickly as she saw the alarmed look on Irene Mullins's face. 'This is a National Trust property and it is possible to visit, but it was a question of time so the itinerary planners back at Super Sun decided to make this a photo stop only.'

'Thank goodness for that. I can't stand heights,' said Joan Fletcher with some feeling.

'The guidebook said this was a good spot to see basking sharks, dolphins and porpoises, but I can't see any sign of them,' said Beryl gazing out to sea.

'I'm afraid if there are any out there, these choppy waters will make them very difficult to spot, but you can see there are lots of kittiwakes nesting on the island and straight ahead I can see some guillemots,' said Fiona stretching out her arm to point them out.

After ten minutes or so when the group had finished taking all the photos they wanted, the wind drove most of them back onto the bus to wait in comfort. Fiona was left with Joan Fletcher waiting for Greg who had moved further along towards the top of the steep steps down to the start of the bridge. He was still scanning the cliffs with his binoculars.

'Greg's a keen birdwatcher, I'm afraid. I'll go and get him back.'

Fiona put a hand on her arm. 'Let's give him a few more minutes. I'm sure the others won't mind waiting. This is supposed to be a great spot for birds.'

'See anything special?' Joan asked when he returned.

'A colony of razorbills and there are quite a few fulmars flying around.'

Fiona ushered the couple on to the coach and picked up the microphone. 'Now we're going to continue along the coast to Ballycastle, and I'll tell you a little more about its famous horse fair when we get there.'

Fiona followed the last of her passengers back into the hotel stifling a yawn. The combination of their excellent substantial lunch followed by the soporific effect of the lengthy coach drive back had made her lethargic, but she must not forget to get in touch with the police officer in charge of trying to find Chester. She'd been given his number when she'd phoned in to report him missing in Rory's office yesterday morning, but she'd left the slip of paper on which she'd written the number up in her room. It was hardly urgent and perhaps a quick cup of tea in the café first might wake her up.

She had only taken a few steps into the foyer when she noticed a man who looked a little out of place in his dark blue suit walking swiftly towards her.

'Mrs Mason?'

'That's me.'

He smiled and held out his hand. Fiona shook it, looking at him expectantly. Without saying anything further, he led her to a couple of chairs well away from listening ears.

'My name is Detective Constable O'Leary.'

'Is this about Chester Porter? Actually, I was about to ring the officer in charge of the case, I…' her voice trailed away as she saw the look on his face.

'A body has been found and we think it could be that of your missing passenger. I'm sorry to have to ask you, madam, but would you mind accompanying me to the mortuary? We need someone who might be able to identify him and I'm afraid there is no one else.'

Fiona felt her mouth go dry. She clasped the arms of the chair, swallowed hard and took a deep breath. Her tote bag slipped from her lap and fell to the floor.

'Would you like me to fetch a glass of water?'

She shook her head, not yet trusting herself to speak. He bent down pushing the half-spilled contents back into the bag as Fiona sat still staring down at her feet, hands still glued to the arms of the chair.

'Tea. I'll order you some tea.' He jumped up and hurried to the desk and was back almost before Fiona's heart had time to return to normal.

Fifteen

Strains of the slow movement of Mendelssohn's Violin Concerto in E minor filled the room, but it was not the majesty of the music of the composer's last large orchestral work that filled his thoughts. Montgomery-Jones picked up the brandy glass from the small table beside his chair and swirled the contents before taking a long sip.

Andrew Salmon had promised to ring him the moment he had confirmation of the dead man's identity. It was already half-way through the evening. What could be keeping the man?

Not for the first time, Montgomery-Jones picked up the phone and then dropped it back onto its cradle. If Salmon had not rung, it was because he had nothing to tell him. Montgomery-Jones drummed his fingers on the well-padded arm of the leather button back chair then suddenly seized the remote control and clicked off the music.

He got to his feet and walked to the window, which looked down into the attractive enclosed gardens. Its peace and serenity was one of the reasons he had bought the property in the first place. This evening, its calming effects were lost to him. He paced through the spacious flat from one room to the next. There was always an overnight bag packed in readiness. He had already taken it from its usual place in the wardrobe and placed it by his bed.

He knew it was not logical. Whatever the information Salmon's Chief Superintendent Dailey would eventually pass on, it could not justify Montgomery-Jones's presence in Belfast, but that did not curb his every inclination to fly out there straightaway.

He crossed to his study-cum-library and switched on his PC. It would not hurt to look at the times of flights. The last British Airways flight from Heathrow was at 19:55 and the Aer Lingus flight was even earlier. There was nothing he could do tonight. Perhaps he should book the first morning flight. There was one at 07.10, which would get him to Belfast by 08:30. He could always cancel it if the dead body proved to have nothing to do with Fiona's missing passenger. Even if it was, and they had no grounds for suspecting that the man was in any way connected to the shooting of Eamon McCollum, he would have a difficult task persuading the Chief that his trip was justified. The case was not within MI6's remit.

On the other hand, he was due some leave. There was currently nothing urgent on his desk. Explaining the lack of notice of his sudden leave might prove somewhat tricky, but he could deal with that when he returned.

His finger was hovering over the confirm booking button when the phone rang.

Fiona sat in the small room nursing yet another cup of tea only half-listening to what the WPC sitting beside her was saying.

'Detective Inspector Flannery will be here in a minute or two if you're up to answering a couple of questions.'

Fiona let the woman's next few sentences pass her by before asking, 'Can you tell me how Mr Porter died?'

The woman smiled and as though speaking to a child said, 'I'm sure the DI will be able to answer all your questions when he gets here.'

She knew that the WPC was only trying to help, but Fiona was beginning to find the woman's soothing tones condescending and wished the woman would just stop talking.

'Drink your tea. It will help with the shock.'

Fiona obediently raised the cup to her lips and took a sip. Her stomach recoiled. Laced with sugar, the milky liquid disguised what taste of tea the brew might once have had. Is this how the relatives of her deceased patients felt when she had been the one offering the tea and sympathy all those years ago in her nursing days? She offered them all a silent prayer of apology.

It was a further ten minutes before the Inspector appeared. He shook her hand and introduced himself. He pulled out a chair tucked under the table and sat down before taking out a small notebook and pen.

'Do you mind if I take a few particulars?'

Fiona wanted to laugh. What if she said no. How would he react? She told herself to pull herself together. This wasn't the place for childish frivolity. It must be a reaction to the shock.

'Let's start with the formalities. You are Mrs Fiona Mason?'

'I am.'

'You are the tour manager for the Super Sun coach tour visiting Belfast and Northern Ireland?'

She nodded.

'And Mr Chester Porter was a passenger on this tour?'

The list of questions went on and on. When had she last seen him and where; what had he been doing; at what time did she realise he was missing; what did she do to find him? She did her best to be patient, but all this was simply going over the same things Fiona had told the police when she had first reported Chester Porter missing. She knew it was necessary procedure, but that didn't stop it being frustrating.

Eventually, she was able to ask, 'Can you tell me how he died?'

'There will need to be a full post-mortem before that can be established.'

Time to stop being a pathetic middle-aged woman needing to be mollycoddled and take some initiative. 'I am well aware of that, Detective Inspector. Nonetheless, the doctor attending the scene will have given a preliminary cause of death. I appreciate that I am in no way entitled to that information but, having just identified Mr Porter's body, I can confirm that his face showed no signs of a sudden heart attack or stroke.'

The Inspector's eyebrows shot up.

'If, as I suspect, his death was in any way suspicious, you will wish to interview each of my passengers and that *is* my concern.'

'Mrs Mason!'

'I'm sorry, Detective Inspector,' she snapped, not giving him time to continue. 'I have just had to identify the body of someone for whose welfare I was responsible. It has been a long day and before it's over, I will have to inform my company of the situation and more importantly, attempt to allay the fears of the rest of my passengers that Belfast is not a city full of murdering muggers lurking around every corner waiting to pounce on them. You'll forgive me if I have neither the time nor the inclination to observe the niceties of following PC protocol and petty procedure. As I understand it, you have no background information on Mr Porter. I was asked to make discreet enquiries amongst my passengers to find out as much about the man as possible. However, if you want me to pass on the details concerning his family and background that might help with your enquiries, then I would appreciate one or two straight answers from you, Detective Inspector. I do not take kindly to being patronised.'

To say that the Inspector looked a trifle stunned was probably an understatement.

Sixteen

'We won't have a more accurate time of death until after the post mortem which should be tomorrow morning, but the police doctor called out to examine the body thought it was most likely sometime on Tuesday, soon after he went missing,' Salmon informed him.

'Which means that Porter could not have been responsible for shooting Eamon McCollum the next day. Am I to take it therefore, that MI5 have no further interest in Porter or the Super Sun party?'

There was a long pause before Andrew Salmon replied. 'To be honest, Peter, I'm not sure. In theory, yes. But there's something a bit strange about all this. It doesn't quite sound like a mugging gone wrong to me. True the man's wallet was taken, but it appears he was wearing an expensive watch and he had a gold signet ring on the little finger of his left hand and they were still on the body when it was found.'

'Perhaps the muggers were simply keen to get away. It did happen in the middle of the day in what I assume was quite a busy place.'

'True, but then this Chester Porter seems to be a real man of mystery. No one appears to know anything about him. He lived in one of these areas where nobody seems to talk to their neighbours and not one of them could tell the local police anything about him except that he had only moved into Pelham Close four or five weeks ago, and that he kept himself to himself. As far as we know, he has no close family and the neighbours haven't noticed any visitors. So far, the police have no information about where he works. They've drawn a complete blank. Something's not right and I can't help feeling something fishy is going on.'

'No one can be that anonymous,' Montgomery-Jones said firmly. 'There must be tax returns, council tax forms, all sorts of data.'

'Yep, but the police are having difficulty tracking any of it down probably because of the recent change of address.'

'I appreciate there must be a vast number of C Porters living in the Greater Manchester area, but Chester is hardly a common forename. Surely to goodness that must be of some help.'

'You'd have thought so, but so far they haven't traced a single one. Perhaps Chester's not the name on his birth certificate. We both know there are a surprising number of people who go by something other than their given name.'

'What about his car? The Driver and Vehicle Licensing Agency will have information on that. If Porter failed to register his new address with the DVLA, they will be able to furnish you with his old one, which might prove more fruitful.'

'It would if he'd had one. A car I mean. Which it seems he didn't. The garage attached to the house was full of boxes. There were unpacked boxes full of stuff all through the house. Only one bedroom and the kitchen were clear and even in there they found only the bare essentials. One plate and set of cutlery, a couple of saucepans and a microwave. The man doesn't appear to have made time to unpack after the move yet. My men are going through the boxes in the hope of finding some personal papers, but it's going to take time?'

Montgomery-Jones moved the phone to his other ear giving himself time to think. 'What about the removal firm he used? They would be able to tell you the man's previous address.'

'None of the local companies have delivered to Pelham Close. We've extended the search area, but he could have come from anywhere in the country. None of the neighbours noticed a removals lorry let alone one with a name on the side. We've tried the van hire places but none reported any customers by the name of Porter.'

'I presume there was no mobile discovered on the body.'

'Nope. Which could be suspicious in itself. Mobiles are highly portable, but it's almost as though the muggers, if that's what they were, were trying to hide the man's identity.'

'What do you intend to do next?'

'My time and resources are fully occupied with the Eamon McCollum's shooting. I'm juggling so many balls right now, I can't afford to pick up another one. My informant is about to chicken out, but I can't drop everything just to go over and hold his hand. Of course, the local police in Belfast will go through the motions, interviewing the Super Sun passengers and the like, but I doubt that it's their number one priority any more than it is mine. The city is currently on a knife-edge. I'm not suggesting that attempting to track down those responsible for the death of a tourist isn't important, but with so little to go on, I think they are pretty stymied.'

'You do not sound happy about the situation.'

'Damned right I'm not. I can't put my finger on it, but there has to be a connection. I can feel it in my water. What if this mysterious Chester Porter is really Edward Masterson? He approximately the same height, build and age.'

'Anything is possible.'

'Do you think I'm on a hide into nothing with this? Honest answer, Peter. Tell me I'm wasting my time with it.'

'I am not certain that you are. My instinct is to agree with you. It would be irresponsible to ignore the possibility. The whole situation needs to be investigated more fully.'

'That's what I hoped you'd say. I don't suppose...' Salmon's voice tailed away

'Go on.'

There was a long pause before Salmon continued. 'I was

going to ask if you would consider a joint operation.'

A slow smile spread across Montgomery-Jones's face. 'It would be difficult to justify. Northern Ireland is British territory. MI6 has no mandate to operate in Belfast.'

'Oh, I don't know,' Salmon adopted a disaffected tone. 'I'm sure you have *some* grounds for suspecting Chester Porter might be liaising with activists south of the border in Ireland?'

Montgomery-Jones chuckled. 'Quite possibly.'

'Will you send someone over there? I think they are more likely to find evidence over in Belfast than working from here. The thing is I also need someone out there who could persuade my informant to carry on working for us. It's more important than ever to get some idea of what's happening now McCollum is out of the picture. We've had sweet fanny adams, absolutely zilch, from him since McCollum was shot.'

'Surely that is a task for his handler?'

'That's the point. He doesn't have one. He reports directly to me.'

'Is that not somewhat unusual?'

'He's a republican. He doesn't trust anyone. Least of all anyone in Belfast.'

'So how did you manage to recruit him in the first place?'

'Like a lot of these things. Pure chance. Being in the right place at the right time. I was in Belfast when Philip Masterson was killed in a so-called hit-and-run. Everyone knew exactly who was responsible. We pulled out all the stops but couldn't prove a damned thing. Anyway, in the process of all those enquiries, we got a hint that at least one of McCollum's cell was not happy. I made it my business to be around one night when he was drinking to hide his sorrows. He was shall we say, somewhat indiscreet. Nothing that serious, but enough to allow me to put a little gentle pressure on him. Since then, I've helped him out of a few tight spots, and he's passed on the odd useful piece of information. Nothing big, except for this last time about the arms in the lockup. Now he's running scared just when he could be worth all the effort that I've spent nurturing him.'

'Tell me more about him. What does he do for a living?'

'Taxi driver. Mid-forties. Been with McCollum and his cronies since just after the Peace Agreement was signed. As I said, I've been running him for nearly three years. The thing is, it's more important than ever to know what's happening in the CIRA now that McCollum's dead. Who's jockeying to take over and what their plans are. Some of these younger ones are more interested in moving into arms smuggling rather than letting off the odd bomb to make a political statement. I'd go myself but my informant's dug his heels in; he just won't talk to me anymore.'

'I see. You are giving my man a complicated brief.' Montgomery-Jones let the silence hang for a good minute. 'On reflection, I wonder if it might be more prudent if I were to go myself.'

Montgomery-Jones was well aware that he was being manipulated. Quite what game Salmon was playing he had no idea. James Fitzwilliam may have exaggerated the hostility between the two services, but there was no denying that the underlying distrust was there. Whatever his MI5 counterpart was up to, for the time being, it suited Montgomery-Jones's plans.

'I hoped you'd say that. I'll let Chief Superintendent Dailey know you're coming. I think he'll be delighted to have help with this. Although a man of his rank wouldn't normally get involved in the day-to-day operation of a case, he's taken a personal interest in what's happening because of the possibly catastrophic fallout if it's allowed to drag on. He's a good man to work with. How soon do you think you can get there?'

'I will leave first thing tomorrow.'

Montgomery-Jones put down the phone and sat leaning on one elbow, pensively drumming the fingers of his other hand on the Regency walnut desk.

Fiona sat next to the Inspector in the back of the unmarked police car and was driven back to the hotel by the same DC O'Leary who had taken her to the mortuary. The Inspector was eager to interview her passengers as soon as possible. Fiona doubted that he would learn anything more than she had already told him, but at least it was reassuring to know that the police were making an effort to find Chester's killer. More importantly, it meant that the responsibility for telling everyone about his death had now passed to the Inspector, for which she was grateful. True, she would have to pick up its aftermath, but she could worry about their reactions later.

As they got out of the car, the Inspector turned to Fiona and said, 'One person you didn't mention was your driver.'

'Winston? What about him?'

'Could he have any information about Chester Porter?'

'I very much doubt it.' Winston was not unobservant – quite the opposite – but he rarely had much opportunity to speak to passengers. Besides, if he'd noticed anything, he would have told her.

'I shall need to speak to him nonetheless.'

'Fine. I'll ring him now and let him know.'

Winston answered straightaway.

'Would you like him to come now? The passengers will still be having dinner.'

'That will be satisfactory.'

Fiona passed on the message and ended the call.

Once inside, the Inspector strode over to the reception desk. The receptionist disappeared into a door behind her but reappeared a moment or two later accompanied by Rory.

After a brief discussion, the Inspector returned to Fiona waiting with DC O'Leary.

'The under-manager is arranging for us to have a private room where we can interview each of your passengers.'

The Inspector took his Detective Constable aside, well out of her hearing, leaving her standing alone in the middle of the lobby. She wasn't sure whether or not she was now free to go. A few moments later, Rory walked over to the two policemen followed by one of the receptionists.

'If you two gentlemen would like to accompany this young lady, she will show you to the room I have arranged for you.'

Once they had disappeared, Rory came to speak to Fiona. 'I take it that Detective Inspector Flannery is the officer in charge of finding your missing passenger?'

'Not quite.'

Rory's habitual friendly open expression took on a bemused look.

Fiona gave a long sigh. 'He's in charge of investigating Chester Porter's murder.'

Rory's eyes widened. He didn't ask for details. He simply reached out and put a hand on her arm and gave a gentle squeeze. 'I am so sorry to hear that. Mrs Mason, if there is anything I can do, anything at all, you only have to ask.'

She had no doubt that he meant every word. It was no conventional meaningless assurance. In the face of relentless, official steamrollering, it was good to know she had an ally.

Dinner was almost over when she went into the restaurant.

'Fiona! There you are. We wondered what had happened to you,' Beryl called out.

Fiona smiled at her and went over to her.

'I'm so sorry about that. I was called away.'

She went round to each of the tables asking them all to wait outside the restaurant doors once they had finished eating.

'You're being very mysterious, Fiona. Is something wrong?' Louise asked.

'I'll explain later, when we're all together. For now, just enjoy the rest of your meal.'

Fiona decided to wait outside. There was no way any of her passengers would let her sit and eat without pestering her with questions. In any case, the superb steak and

Guinness pie followed by a generous portion of Bailey's cheesecake that she'd had at lunchtime were more than enough to satisfy any hunger pangs, so missing another full meal was no hardship. Besides which, she had completely lost her appetite.

She slumped into the nearest chair and closed her eyes. What a day!

The group sat huddled in a tight semi-circle facing the Inspector and Fiona placed herself slightly behind him but well to the side.

'Ladies and gentlemen, I regret to inform you that the body of Chester Porter was found earlier today…'

The Inspector's next words were drowned out by shocked exclamations. Irene gave a high-pitched squeak and pulled out a handkerchief dapping her eyes. Beside her, Norman sat wide-eyed and open-mouthed. Beryl turned and buried her head into her husband's chest whilst he ineffectually patted her back. Stephanie's hands flew to her face covering her mouth.

There was a barrage of questions.

'What happened?'

'How did he…?'

'Was it a heart attack?'

The Inspector put up his hands, 'Ladies and gentlemen.'

Gradually the hubbub subsided, and he continued, 'We have yet to determine the details, but we are treating Mr Porter's death as suspicious.'

This produced another flurry of questions.

'Please! Can we have some quiet.' It wasn't a question. The Inspector stood, clenching and unclenching his jaw. 'As you can appreciate, it would help our enquiries considerably if each of you would think back to the day Mr Porter disappeared. I understand from Mrs Mason that you were all together outside the Palm House in the Botanic Gardens at noon or thereabouts when the group split up. Did anyone see Mr Porter after that?'

There was head shaking all round.

'Surely someone spotted him. It's not exactly a huge area.'

'There were a lot of people in the gardens,' said Louise. 'Once we all went our separate ways, everyone disappeared into the crowd.'

'Most of us headed out of the park to look for somewhere to have lunch. I know I did,' said Stephanie. 'I don't think I saw any of the others till we met back at the meeting place at two o'clock.'

There were nods all round.

'Where exactly was the body found, Inspector?'

'I am not at liberty to tell you the exact location.'

The Inspector asked a few more questions but it was all too evident that no one had anything of value to pass on. 'In which case ladies and gentlemen, if no one has any more information to give us, I will leave you. Thank you for your time. I do urge you to think over the events leading up to Mr Porter going missing and if you do recall anything, however seemingly insignificant, please do not hesitate to get in touch, either directly or through Mrs Mason.'

Once Detective Inspector Flannery and Detective Constable O'Leary had left the room, the excited chatter began again.

'It seems strange to me that a man could be mugged and left for dead with all those people around.' Colin's voice rose above the others.

'Is that what happened?' asked Irene. 'The Inspector didn't say he was mugged.'

'What else could it be? Who'd want to kill Chester?'

Irene's eyes swivelled briefly in Greg's direction.

'I need a stiff drink.' David Cox walked to the door and one by one the others followed.

Day 6 Friday

Today we have a full-day tour taking us on a coastal drive to enjoy the rugged cliff scenery of the Antrim coast up to the magnificent Queen of the Glens, Glenariff and the Glenariff Forest Park. The picturesque valleys of the nine Glens radiate from the Antrim Plateau to the coast and are an area of outstanding natural beauty.

As we drive north from Belfast, we will see majestic rugged cliffs and each bend in the road will give us stunning views with dramatic headlands and bays. We will pass through pretty villages nestled in charming little bays such as the small fishing port of Carnlough.

The town of Larne is believed to get its name from Prince Lathar, son of an ancient Irish king, who was granted the lands by his father.

North of Larne is the village of Ballygally with its seventeenth century Scottish baronial castle overlooking the sea, which is now a hotel. The castle is reputed to host a number of ghosts.

Glenariff Forest Park covers an area of 2,900 acres of which 2,200 acres have been planted with trees. The remainder consists of several small lakes, recreation areas and open space left for landscape and conservation reasons. Bisecting the Park are two small but beautiful rivers: the Inver and the Glenariff, each containing spectacular waterfalls, tranquil pools and stretches of fast-flowing water tumbling through rocky steep-sided gorges.

We will have some free time to walk in the park before visiting the Tea Rooms.

Our drive back to the hotel will follow the route inland through Ballymena.

Super Sun Executive Travel

Seventeen

'I lay awake last night worrying about it. I know it's ridiculous, but my mind just kept coming back to the expression on his face.'

'Just 'cause he's got a temper, don't make him a killer.'

'I know that, Winston. That's exactly what I kept telling myself. It's preposterous to even consider Greg as a murderer. Besides, if he was really that angry, why would he wait so long? It doesn't make sense.'

'Exactly. Most like, it was a mugging gone wrong. If that Inspector chappie suspected any of our lot, they'd be hauling us off to the nearest police station to grill us all.'

'The thing is, should I tell the Inspector about what happened on the ferry or not?'

'That's up to you, sweetheart.'

'If I do, he'll probably accuse me of withholding evidence for not telling him when Chester first went missing.'

Winston shrugged his massive shoulders.

'If Greg did do it, he's a pretty good actor. Last night when the Inspector gave everyone the news, he looked genuinely shocked.' Fiona stirred her tea momentarily lost in thought. 'I'll tell you something else that's a bit odd, Winston. When I asked Chester about his parents, he said they lived down on the south coast, but the thing is, he told Irene that his only relation was an older sister now living in Australia.'

'Perhaps, he don't get on with his parents.'

'Possibly. He did seem very reticent to talk about them.'

'Why don't you have your breakfast now and decide what you're going to tell the Inspector later? You'll think better on a full stomach.'

She looked across at the silver dishes lined up on the hot counter on the far side of the room. 'I have to confess, not having eaten since lunch yesterday, I'm feeling quite peckish this morning.

Winston frowned. 'Now don't you go skipping meals. You need to keep your strength up.'

'I'm fine, Winston. I really wasn't hungry.'

'I suppose not after what they put you through. They shouldn't have asked you to identify that body. If I'd have known when I spoke to him, I'd have given that Inspector a piece of my mind.'

'Nobody forced me. And I've seen enough dead bodies in my time and,' she said ruefully, 'not just in my nursing days! Having worked in emergency and in surgery, I can assure you, there are far more gruesome sights than a body after it's been washed and laid out in the morgue. Still let's change the subject. I haven't asked you about your interview with the Inspector.'

She'd had every intention of finding Winston last evening after the Inspector had left, but the Inspector's news had left everyone shocked and she had needed to be there for her passengers. One way and another, it had been quite late before she'd got to her room.

'Bit of a waste of time. Still, they have to go through the motions I suppose.'

'I think the main problem is that they can't find out anything about him. They have his address and that's about it.'

'Bit odd, ain't it?' Winston frowned.

'You can say that again. From something the Inspector let slip yesterday when I overheard him talking on his mobile, I think the police are trying to make a connection between Chester Porter and the shooting of the prisoner at the hospital the other day. Though what their deaths have in common, I can't fathom. Chester might have been a bit of a mystery man, but I can't see him as an Irish terrorist somehow.'

'So how did the passengers take it?'

'Most of them overreacted if you ask me. I expected Irene and Beryl to be upset and perhaps it was their response that prompted the others, but it all felt a bit too staged for my liking. They behaved as though they'd lost a close friend, but they'd known Chester for little more than a day. Half of them had admitted earlier that they'd exchanged no more than a casual greeting with him.'

'If he was mugged, perhaps it was their own safety they were worried about.'

'You're probably right.' She gave a long sigh. 'I suppose that's the obvious explanation.'

'You don't sound convinced.'

'Belfast may have had its troubles in the past, but these days it's reckoned to be a relatively safe place for tourists.'

'Has anyone said they wanna leave the tour and go back home?'

'I think everyone was much too shocked last night to even think about it. We'll see how things go today. That's why I'd like to keep them all occupied as much as possible. There is a tendency for some people to feed on the hysteria of others, so I'd like not to give them too much time to chat together. I'm tempted to shorten the morning coffee and lunch breaks. What do you think?'

'You's in charge, sweetheart. I don't have a problem with it.'

'Let's play it by ear.'

'Sounds good to me.'

Fiona picked up the microphone. 'In a few minutes, we'll be driving into Ballygally where we're going to make a short photo stop so that you can take pictures of the four-hundred-year old castle. It's the oldest 17th century building still used as a residence in Northern Ireland today. I'm sure you've all read the information in your tour programmes and you'll already know that the castle is said to be haunted.'

'Isn't it a hotel nowadays?' asked Irene. 'I'm not sure I'd like to stay in a place where there are supposed to be ghosts.'

Fiona laughed. 'That seems to be the main attraction for many people, apart from its lovely views of course. The story goes that Lady Isobel Shaw fell to her death from the window after her husband had locked her in her room and starved her. She has a habit of knocking on doors and disappearing.'

'Well that's one way to frighten people,' said Louise.

'I can just see a couple of naughty kids creeping around late at night and causing havoc,' said her husband much to the amusement of those around him.

'There is another ghost said to be that of a Madame Nixon who lived in the hotel in the 19th century. The eerie rustling of her silk skirts can be heard as she walks the corridors. There's a small room in the corner turret of the castle known as "The Ghost Room" but it's not used as a guest room.'

When they came to a halt, everyone got off to take pictures.

'Can't say it looks much like a castle to me,' muttered Greg Fletcher to his wife. 'Apart from those round towers at each corner, it could be any old building.'

Greg's judgement seemed to be the consensus, and, after the single obligatory picture, he and the rest of the group turned back to the dramatic views along the coastline and the small bay, which certainly did merit a photograph or two.

Fiona stood to one side using the opportunity to survey the group. No one had mentioned Chester to her as they had congregated in the foyer before the start of the tour and nor had she heard anyone talking about the dreadful revelations of last evening. In fact, Fiona thought, as she looked around, everyone seemed to have completely forgotten about their deceased fellow passenger. Most of them looked happy enough. She glanced at Greg, but he was busy surveying the coastline with his binoculars and it was impossible to read his face. As far as she could tell, from the way he'd been behaving the last day or so, any grudges he'd held against Chester had long since disappeared.

There had been no seats on the early morning flight to Belfast, which, on reflection Montgomery-Jones decided, was probably not such a bad thing. There was sufficient time to go into Vauxhall Cross before the taxi arrived to take him to Heathrow. It meant that he was able to ask James Fitzwilliam to sort out one or two outstanding matters and to keep his PA up to date with what was happening.

Although his senior position meant that he did not need to inform the Director General of his decision to be away from his desk prior to leaving, he decided it would be politic to send a memo giving the man a brief explanation for his absence for the next few days at the request of MI5.

When he arrived at Belfast airport, he went first to the hotel and once he had checked in, he took a taxi to the police station. It was almost lunchtime when he arrived.

Although no specific time had been arranged, Chief Superintendent Dailey was expecting him, so he was shown into the man's office almost immediately. The big barrel-chested man in his early fifties who arose from the chair cut an impressive figure in his smart uniform. He came forward offering a warm smile and an outstretched hand.

'Welcome to Belfast.'

The handshake was firm and any fears that Montgomery-Jones might have harboured that his presence might be seen as an unwelcome intrusion were quickly dispersed.

'As I'm sure you appreciate, the shooting of Eamon McCollum could have major repercussions. The whole city is on a knife-edge. Feelings are high. Unless we get a lid on it and soon, Belfast could ignite into the worst sectarian violence we've had since the Troubles. We've already had a couple of incidents. Nothing major as yet, although there was an attempt to blow up a prominent Protestant social club, but, thanks to good surveillance work, we managed to foil the operation and made several arrests.'

'That is good to know.'

'All police leave has been cancelled, I've put every available man I have on the streets and called for more officers to be brought in from other districts.'

'I do understand the seriousness of the situation. That is why you can be assured of every assistance the Security Services can give.'

'To be frank, so far we've made little progress on this McCollum case.'

'Andrew Salmon said you were experiencing difficulties. Have you no suspects?'

Chief Superintendent Dailey gave a bitter laugh. 'Hundreds. They're crawling out of the woodwork. That's the problem. We've eliminated many of the more likely ones, but now we've drawn a blank.'

'Salmon appears convinced that Edward Masterson could well be the culprit.'

'So he keeps telling me.'

'Am I to take it that you are not persuaded?'

The Chief Superintendent shrugged. 'He's as good a suspect as any given that Salmon and his team haven't managed to trace Edward Masterson's whereabouts. We're not ruling him out, but let's just say he is not at the top of our list.'

Montgomery-Jones sat back in his chair and crossed his legs. 'What about this tourist, Chester Porter? In your opinion, could the two deaths be linked?'

'Who knows? DI Flannery will give you a copy of the post-mortem report. He's in charge of that investigation and can tell you far more about the progress so far. I'll take you to meet him after lunch. Just a few sandwiches, if that's okay?'

Montgomery-Jones smiled and nodded and both men got to their feet.

'While we eat, I'll bring you up to speed on the details on this case.'

There were various trails in Glenariff Forest Park and once they left the visitor centre, many of the more active of her passengers headed straight for the Waterfall Trail.

Fiona noticed Norman and Irene Mullins standing by the information board looking at the map.

'We're not quite certain which to do, Fiona,' confessed Irene.

'I suppose it depends on how energetic you are feeling. The waterfalls are truly spectacular. The trail is only a couple of miles, but it is very steep. Which is fine going down, but you do have to come back up again. Not that the path up the valley side is particularly difficult, it's a proper wooden boardwalk, but it does have a great many steps.'

'Hmm.' Norman looked doubtful.

'On the other hand, you could always opt for the Viewpoint Trail. That's only half a mile. From there you'll be able to look down the Glen to the sea in the distance. According to the information literature here,' Fiona showed them the leaflet. 'The walk then takes you past the café and back to the car park via the ornamental gardens.'

Norman's face brightened. 'That sounds more like our cup of tea. Isn't that where we are all meeting up again? At the café.'

'That's right. If you have any spare time, you might like to take a look at the exhibition centre.'

Detective Inspector Flannery was short, thick-set but fit-looking, and not far off retirement. He too had a firm handshake and though his tone was friendly, Montgomery-Jones detected a degree of suspicion in the man's eyes.

Once the preliminaries were over, the two men got down to business.

'Chief Superintendent Dailey tells me that Her Majesty's Security Services believe there's a link between the death of this tourist and the shooting of Eamon McCollum? Is that right?'

'That is putting it far too strongly. It is only one of many possibilities. It might assist the investigation into the McCollum case if we could rule out any link, so it seemed logical to discuss it with you.'

'I see.' DI Flannery appeared a little more mollified. 'Well, Chester Porter's death certainly wasn't a straightforward mugging gone wrong, we're certain of that. If you want to take a man's wallet, you don't creep up behind him and stick a knife in his back first.'

'Was the knife left with the body?'

Flannery shook his head. 'No. And nothing like that was found anywhere near where the body was found.'

'There were no other injuries?'

'Only those consistent with someone kneeling on him when he fell, presumably to hold him down and he had something clamped over his mouth to stop him calling out. They found fibres in his nose and throat.

'Did you learn anything useful from the interviews with the other passengers on the tour?'

'Not really. Apparently, they were all left to their own devices for a couple of hours outside the Palm House at the Botanical Gardens and no one saw him after.'

'Were they able to tell you anything about his background?'

'Nothing more than the tour manager had given us before. I understand you know this Fiona Mason?'

Montgomery-Jones gave a knowing smile. 'Our paths have crossed a few times.'

'Formidable lady.'

'She can be a little forthright, shall we say.'

Flannery raised an eyebrow. 'You ever been on the end of her tongue-lashing?'

Montgomery-Jones gave a long sigh. 'More times than I care to remember.'

The Inspector gave him a conspiratorial smile. Thanks to

Fiona, Detective Inspector Flannery's ice barrier was beginning to melt.

Eighteen

It was almost six o'clock when the coach arrived back at the hotel. Fiona decided to dump her things in her room and go straight down to one of the lounge areas and order a pot of tea. Not that she was particularly thirsty, but she wanted to sit quietly and take a rest somewhere pleasant where she could watch the world go by for a quarter of an hour before getting ready for dinner.

There were some magazines laid out on one of the tables and Fiona picked one up. She was idly flicking through its pages as she sipped her tea, when footsteps approached.

'Good evening, Fiona.'

Fiona looked up with a start, almost spilling her tea.

'Peter! What are you doing here?'

'I was hoping I might find you at this time of day. Do you mind if I join you?' He folded himself into the comfortable chair next to hers. 'So how have you been keeping since I last saw you? Well I trust.'

'Yes, thank you,' she muttered, before burying her nose in her cup.

'It seems some time ago now.' His voice betrayed no hurt, but then he'd never been an easy man to read. Unlike her, who wore her emotions on her sleeve, for most of the time, it was impossible to tell what Peter was thinking or feeling.

Fiona's mouth went dry and she could feel the heat rising to her cheeks as she replayed the last few moments of their previous meeting. It had been a wonderful evening up until that point. A superb meal in a Michelin star restaurant. She could still taste the Grand Marnier in the soufflé so light that it had almost melted in her mouth.

They had just returned from a stressful tour to Berlin and the Elbe Valley. Unbeknownst to her until the end, Peter had manipulated Super Sun into arranging for her to be the tour guide on the trip on which he had been working undercover posing as one of her passengers. Relations between them throughout the two weeks had been stressful to put it mildly. When they returned to London, he had suggested taking her for a meal by way of making up for the friction.

Throughout the meal, Peter had been at his most charming. There were times in the past – many, many times – when she had been driven to distraction by his pompous arrogance, but she had never denied that even with the now-silver hair, he was also one of the most handsome men she had ever known. He only had to give her that smile of his to make her stomach flip like some silly schoolgirl. The problem was he probably knew it. Nonetheless, it had been a magical evening. She had never felt herself so close to him. She hadn't wanted the evening to end.

They sat for so long, lingering over coffee that she was in danger of missing the last train back home to Guildford. He had paid the bill and they collected Fiona's luggage. As he walked her to the door, he offered to drive her home.

But what would happen then? Would he invite himself in? Suddenly she wasn't sure if she was ready for this. She panicked. There was a taxi outside the hotel, and on impulse, she had replied that she couldn't possibly put him to the trouble of driving her all that way. She had thanked him for the evening and jumped into the taxi asking the driver to take her to Waterloo station before Peter had had a chance to reply.

The next day, she knew she ought to ring and apologise for the abruptness of her departure, but she couldn't face it. What could she possibly say? Instead, she sent him a short email, thanking him for the delicious meal and apologising for rushing off, explaining that she'd wanted to seize the taxi before it sped away. He had acknowledged her email, written that he had enjoyed her company and that they should do it again sometime. Too embarrassed to reply, she had tried to forget all about the evening, telling herself that their paths would never cross again.

And yet here he was. Sitting right next to her. Within touching distance! At least she had a few moments to recover, as he looked around for a waiter.

Once Peter had ordered, deciding to get in first, she said, 'What brings you to Belfast? Are you involved in the terrorist shooting case?'

'Amongst other things. You have been having a few problems on your tour, I understand.'

She was well aware that he was looking at her, attempting to hold her gaze, but she wasn't quite ready to look straight into his eyes just yet. She picked up her cup again. 'You could say that. So how did you find out?'

'I have just been speaking to Detective Inspector Flannery.'

'Oh?'

'He remarked on how forthright you were.'

'Did he now?' she growled.

Peter chuckled. 'He also commented on how astute you appeared to be.'

'How good of him.' Fiona tried to keep the sarcasm from her voice. 'So, if you are in Belfast looking into the shooting of Eamon McCollum, how come you've been talking with Detective Inspector Flannery?'

'Inspectors are concerned with more than one case at a time.'

'If my name came up, then you were obviously discussing Chester Porter. What have your investigations to do with the mugging of one of my passengers?'

He didn't reply straight away. 'If you ever get bored working for Super Sun, Mrs Mason, you must come and work for me. Your interrogation techniques are admirable.

Nothing gets past you.'

'I've learnt from the master. And you still haven't answered my question.'

He chuckled. 'Honest answer. I would like to be certain that there is nothing to connect the two cases.'

'I don't understand. Why should there be?'

'Two deaths around the same time a short distance from one another, it would be negligent not to consider the possibility.'

'Which means you are here to interview me?'

'Not at all. I came to look for a friend to say hello.'

She gave him a sheepish grin. 'Sorry. Old habits die hard.'

'Perhaps it is time you took me at my word and stopped looking for some hidden motive behind our meetings. Tell me, how are you enjoying Belfast? What have you seen so far?'

It wasn't until she saw Peter again sitting at a table by himself at the far end of the restaurant facing the Super Sun tables, that she realised he must be staying in the hotel. He hadn't mentioned it earlier, but they had had little time to talk as she'd had to leave to get ready for dinner. He was still formally dressed, but, although the majority of the hotel's guests were tourists, there were sufficient businessmen booked into the hotel that he didn't look totally out of place.

'I loved that little fishing village we went through on the way up to the Glens. What was it called, Fiona?' Beryl asked.

'Do you mean Carnlough?'

'That's it. I really must write it down. We visit so many places and take so many photos, when you get home and look through them all again, it's hard to remember exactly where they were unless you make a record straight away.'

The seating of the hotel's Sonoma restaurant was laid out with small tables of four which meant that Fiona had to push all thoughts of her recent exchange with Peter from her mind and join in the conversation. At least, sitting with the Coxes, Beryl could be relied upon to keep up the discussion. For most of the time, all Fiona had to do was nod in the right places and make the occasional comment.

There were so many questions she wished she'd asked Peter. Knowing him, he'd probably be his normal evasive self, but that wouldn't stop her trying. She'd been so surprised to see him, and too busy trying to hide her embarrassment, to even think about quizzing him at the time.

'Fiona?'

'I'm so sorry. I was miles away. What did you say, David?'

'I only asked if you were planning on going out tonight. I know several of the younger people are heading out.'

'Probably not. I have a lot of paperwork to catch up on. Are you two thinking of joining them?'

'But do you think it's a good idea to go at all after what happened to poor Chester?' Beryl clearly did not relish the idea.

'That policeman who came to talk to us didn't say not to,' her husband tried to reassure her.

'I think it's probably more sensible to go in small groups rather than on your own. Not that I think for a moment that anything might happen, I wouldn't suggest it otherwise, but it will make you feel safer,' Fiona added.

'I'm feeling rather tired anyway.' Beryl was not to be persuaded.

Perhaps it was time to change the subject. 'I'm looking forward to going to Mount Stewart House tomorrow. I'm going to let you into a little secret,' Fiona said conspiratorially, 'I've never been before, but it sounds magnificent.'

'I'm sure it is, but one of the reasons we chose to come on this particular trip is the Game of Thrones tour on the last day. David and I never miss an episode, do we, pet?' She didn't wait for his reply before leaning forward and dropping her voice, she continued. 'I was talking with Irene and it seems she and Norman are avid fans too.'

'I've heard it is extremely popular.'

Beryl laughed. 'You've never watched it, have you, Fiona?'

'Well, no. I don't have Sky television. I always imagined that the majority of its fans were teenagers and young people. Isn't it a medieval fantasy?'

'Yes, but it's very violent. And *very* graphic. People get their heads chopped off all the time. What's more, it's extremely raunchy. Not the sort of thing you'd expect two respectable old dears like them to watch.'

'We like it because it's so unpredictable,' said her husband. 'You never know what's going to happen next. You daren't miss an episode because even one of the main characters might suddenly be killed. We've had to record it while we're away otherwise we'd lose the plot completely by the time we got back.'

Her mobile started to ring as she left the restaurant.

'Hello.'

'Fiona, it's David Rushworth. I've just been speaking to Allan Trent. It was his name and number Chester Porter put down as his emergency contact.'

'The one you couldn't get through to.

'That's it. He's contacted us. Seems he'd been ringing Porter's mobile for several days and getting no answer so decided to get in touch with us for the details of the hotel where Porter was staying. I had to tell him what happened.'

'Oh dear.'

'Not exactly a pleasant task. The man was almost hysterical. I managed to calm him down in the end. Anyway, the upshot is that he says he'll becoming over to Belfast tomorrow. He wants to take the body back home.'

'I see.'

'I've already informed Belfast police.'

'Thank you for that.'

The Tours Director rang off and Fiona returned her mobile to her pocket with a long, drawn-out sigh. Just what she needed! As if she didn't have enough to cope with without having Chester's hysterical friend to add to the mix.

Nineteen

The first thing she needed to do was to find Peter. She tried his mobile, but all she got was a recorded message saying the person she was trying to call was busy right now and she should leave a message. She hesitated for a moment or two then decided to ring off. Not that she thought he wouldn't get back to her. He'd given no indication that he wanted to avoid her. Whatever her reaction to meeting again, it was clear that he harboured no grudge for her abrupt departure in London three months ago.

She needed to speak to him face to face. It was the only way she was going to get any answers out of him. He had never given her an adequate explanation of why he thought there might be a link between the two deaths.

She'd assumed, because she'd seen him at dinner, that he was staying in the hotel, but he hadn't said so. She could ask at the desk of course. As he was not one of her party, there was a good chance that the receptionist would be reluctant to tell her. Hotels had become much less free with such information in recent years since all the fuss about the individual's right to personal privacy and the growing trend of a few people to sue institutions on the slightest of grounds. She could always ask Rory. He seemed to have a soft spot for her and might be persuaded.

Perhaps she should start with a quick look around the bars and lounge areas. She found Peter almost straight away. He was standing by the window, facing out onto the street below, his mobile still held to his ear. She waited, hovering in the doorway, until he'd finished. The last thing she wanted was for him to think she was trying to listen in to his conversation.

He turned and saw her.

'I came to tell you the news about Chester Porter's friend, but I'm guessing that was what your phone call was about.'

He nodded and to her surprise, instead of rushing away, motioned her to a chair. 'Would you like a drink? I was about to get one for myself.'

'Not for me, thank you.'

Once he'd settled himself into the seat next to her, she said, 'The Tours Director at Super Sun told me that Allan Trent is coming over tomorrow.'

'So I understand. Have you any idea of what time? The police will want to interview him, plus they will need him to officially identify the body.'

'Give the poor man a chance. He's only just learnt that his friend is dead. I would imagine he's still in a state of shock. I don't suppose he's had a chance to even look up the flight times yet.'

'Exactly.' He smiled. 'Which is why I thought it might be nice for someone to be there when he arrives to help him through what is going to be a pretty gruelling experience?'

'Oh. I'm sorry. I didn't mean to be so sharp.' She sighed and sank back into the chair.

'You look a little exhausted yourself. How are you coping with all this?'

'Me?' She gave a rueful laugh. 'You could say I'm getting used to having to deal with dead bodies and their aftermath on my tours. Though you are right about one thing. Suddenly, I do feel pretty shattered. Too tired to play games, Peter. I confess I would dearly love to know exactly why you are so interested in Chester Porter and what possible connection he could have with the shooting of Eamon McCollum.'

He sighed. 'You know I cannot tell you.'

'That's what I thought you'd say, but it's really bugging

me, Peter. Chester seemed such a nice person. A bit shy. I think he was quite a lonely man. Not a bit like a terrorist.'

'Oh, I doubt he was that.'

'Then why on earth are you so interested in him?'

There was a long pause before Peter said, 'As I told you before, he was something of a mystery man. The police have been unable to establish much about his background or trace anyone who knows him.'

'I rather gathered that when I was asked if he'd said anything to me about his family or about his work. Haven't they spoken to his neighbours?'

'As I understand it, he only moved into the house a few weeks ago.'

'I suppose that's an indictment of our modern society. In the olden days, someone would come knocking on the newcomer's door with offers of help and invitations to pop round for coffee. Nowadays, people barely seem to recognise anyone who lives more than two doors away.'

When he made no comment, she continued, 'I also find it interesting that Detective Inspector Flannery fobbed me off when I asked how he died. He tried to suggest that Chester might have had a sudden heart attack. He quickly realised that the death would be reported in the local press so he knew he wouldn't get away with that. By the time he spoke to the rest of my passengers, he admitted that the circumstances of Chester's death were, to use his word, suspicious. We all assumed, as did the press, that it was as a result of a mugging. A robbery gone wrong. If that were indeed the case, then I see no reason for you to maintain your interest in him. Mystery man or no.'

She waited for some sort of response, but his face remained deadpan.

'I can't help wondering if Chester was deliberately murdered. Which of course begs the question as to why?'

'You have a very vivid imagination, Mrs Mason.' Though his voice remained neutral, she took his use of her surname as a warning.

'No. I'm simply pursuing a logical train of thought.' She gave a laugh and continued theatrically, 'So, was it revenge for something he'd done, was someone trying to stop him doing something or did he know something someone did not want revealed?'

'Or was he simply a man in the wrong place at the wrong time,' he said firmly.

'I did consider that first off, but then I decided against it.'

'Not exciting enough for you?'

'Exactly. Far too prosaic. It would help of course if we knew exactly who stabbed him in the back.'

His eyes suddenly widened. It was only the tiniest of movements and lasted a mere fraction of a second. If she hadn't been looking directly at him, she'd have missed it.

'So that's how he died! Actually, I only meant it as a figure of speech.'

'Shall we stop this game?' Peter's face looked pained.

She nodded and gave a long sigh. 'It might be a great deal more fun if it wasn't a real dead body that we are talking about. Peter, I know you can't break any official regulations or give away any secrets, and I'm not asking you to. But I liked Chester Porter and I know it's illogical, but I do feel responsible for him. When all this is over, will you let me know why he had to die?'

'I will, on condition that we drop the subject now.'

'Deal.'

Peter asked after her grandchildren, Becky and Adam junior who lived out in Canada, and they sat talking for some time.

'I hadn't realised it was so late. It's time I was heading up to my room if I'm going to be bright-eyed and bushy-tailed for my passengers tomorrow morning.'

She noticed one of the dark-suited young men from behind the reception desk coming towards her followed by a slightly dishevelled-looking man in his early- to mid-forties.

'Mrs Mason. This gentleman would like to speak to you,

if that's all right?'

The second man approached her holding out a hand, 'My name is Allan Trent. I'm a friend of Chester Porter. Your boss said you wouldn't mind me having a word when I got here. I know it's late, but…'

After a moment's hesitation, she smiled and shook the proffered hand. 'Of course not. Forgive me. We weren't expecting you until tomorrow morning.'

'I managed to get a flight this evening. I wanted to get here as soon as possible.'

'I see. May I introduce Peter Montgomery-Jones.'

Allan looked doubtfully at the tall man who had risen and was now towering above him.

Peter gave a slight bow of the head and took a step back. 'I will leave you both to discuss matters in private.'

'Don't go, Peter.' She turned to Allan. 'I know you must have a great many questions to ask about what happened to Chester. Peter is involved in the case and I think you might find that he can give you more information than I can.'

'Are you a policeman?'

'No,' Fiona answered for him. 'He is a police consultant. Will that be all right?'

Allan looked uncertain, but he nodded and perched himself on the edge of the chair next to Fiona, clenching his hands between his knees.

Peter, still standing, asked, 'Would you like a coffee or something stronger?'

'Just coffee. That will be fine.'

Once Peter had left, Fiona said, 'I'm so sorry for your loss.'

Every time she heard that expression on American TV shows, she thought how trite and insincere it sounded, but at this moment, she couldn't think of a better way of expressing herself.

'Thank you. It was a great shock.' Allan was already blinking back tears.

'Indeed. Chester seemed such a nice person. I only knew

him a couple of days of course, but we had several chats and we sat together at breakfast one morning. He was utterly charming.'

'He was very special.'

By the time Peter returned with the coffee, Allan had regained his control.

'The man I spoke to at the tour company said that Chester went missing on Tuesday.'

'That's right. We tried the emergency contact number, but it didn't make a connection. There seems to have been a mix-up with the numbers.'

'Chester's writing was always illegible. So, what happened?'

Fiona explained how Chester had failed to arrive after their free time in the Botanic Gardens. 'We waited for him for some time, but he never showed up. When he hadn't returned to the hotel by the evening, I contacted the police. His body wasn't found until yesterday.'

'How did he die?'

'We won't know that until we get the results of the post-mortem, but,' she leant across and put a hand on his arm, 'I should tell you, the police are treating his death as suspicious.'

Allan's hands shot up to cover his face, which did little to muffle the loud wracking sobs that shook his whole body.

Fiona shifted in her chair so that she could wrap her arms around him and rock him like a baby.

Once the noise died down and Fiona released her hold, she said quietly. 'There will need to be a formal identification of the body.'

'But I thought…' Allan turned to stare at her. 'I thought you…'

'I could only vouch for the fact that he was one of my passengers.'

'I'm not sure I…' His bottom lip trembled and for a moment, Fiona thought the sobbing might break out again.

'Is there a member of his family who can be asked?'

Allan wiped a hand over his face. '*I'm* his family.' He clenched his jaw and said more firmly, 'His *only* family. His parents disowned him twenty years ago, when he told them he was gay. They've never spoken since.'

'Had you been together long?' Fiona asked.

'Three years this October. We work... worked for the same company. He was in software design and I'm in the accounts office. Chester didn't want anyone to know he's gay, so we didn't exactly live together. That's his father's fault,' He said with sudden venom. 'He threw Chester out of the house forbidding his mother to have anything to do with him ever again. Cut him off without a penny. That rejection scarred Chester for life. That's why he was so secretive about our relationship. He liked to pretend that no one knew about us at work, but of course, they all did. I couldn't seem to convince him that no one cares about such things these days anyway. He wouldn't even agree to us going on holiday together. We'd go out for odd days, for meals, to concerts and so on, but not where we'd have to mix with other people we might know.'

'That must be difficult for you.'

Allan took out a handkerchief and blew his nose.

'When can I take Chester back home?'

'I really don't know. You will need to ask the police about that. I presume that because of the suspicious nature of his death, they may not wish to release the body straight away.'

'There may also be an added problem.' Both Allan and Fiona turned to look at Peter. 'The authorities are unlikely to allow someone who is not a relative to take charge of the body, especially if either of his parents is still alive. The fact that the two of you have never shared a house together may prove a further complication when you attempt to argue your case.'

Allan's face went from pale to an ashen grey and his whole body sagged even further.

'If, as you say, his parents want nothing to do with him, that may not prove to be an insurmountable problem.'

'There is a sister out in Australia somewhere. They weren't exactly close. They exchanged Christmas cards I believe, but that was pretty much it, as far as I know.'

'There is nothing we can do about that now. It's well past midnight. May I suggest you try to get some rest and we'll sort something out in the morning,' said Fiona.

As they all walked towards the door, Allan suddenly stopped and turned to Fiona, his eyes wide in panic. 'I don't think I can. Not look at his poor dead body just lying there. It's too much.'

'He looks very peaceful.' It was all she could think to say.

'Do you think… I know it's a lot to ask, but could you… would you come with me? Please.' He suddenly clutched Fiona's arm gripping it so tight it was painful.

'If it will help, I'm sure it can be arranged.'

She patted his hand and was rewarded with a weak but grateful smile.

Day 7 Saturday

This morning is free to explore the city at leisure. There are many fascinating places to see including St Anne's Cathedral. The foundation stone of this fine Neo-Romanesque building was laid in 1899 and it was consecrated in 1904. The Spire of Hope was added in 2006. The cathedral's interior is particularly impressive. The wide nave is paved with Canadian maple and the aisles with Irish marble. The stained-glass windows are striking. The cathedral's outstanding feature is the many mosaics. One shows St Patrick's journey to Ireland and another covering the baptistry ceiling is made up of 150,000 separate pieces of stone.

Another popular option is a tour of the Victorian-era Crumlin Road Gaol. The gaol first opened in 1846 and was a fully operational prison for 150 years. It closed in 1996, but in 2012, it became a visitor attraction. A guided tour recounts the history of the gaol and takes in the condemned cell, the execution cell where 17 prisoners were hanged, and which leads through the underground tunnel that connected the gaol to the courthouse.

Our afternoon tour takes us to Mount Stewart House and gardens. This impressive 18th century mansion with its splendid interior is now owned by the National Trust. However, its magnificent gardens are its main attraction. They have been voted one of the world's top ten gardens.

The house used to belong to the Londonderry family, the most famous of whom was Lord Castlereagh. He was Chief Secretary for Ireland and then British Foreign Secretary in the early 1800s.

The house re-opened in 2015 after a three-year seven-million-pound restoration. The house contains many sumptuous rooms, with fine furnishings and rich ornamentation with decorated archways and elaborate ceilings, plus many beautiful treasures including the picture of a celebrated racehorse by George Stubbs that hangs in the main stairway. The Entrance Hall is the most austere room in the house. Its stone pillars have been painted to resemble marble.

The gardens span 98 acres and were planted in the 1920s by Lady Edith, wife of the 7th Marquess of Londonderry. The exotic plants and trees have thrived in the area because of its subtropical microclimate. The Italian Garden, in front of the house, is the largest of the formal gardens. There are several others including the Sunken Garden with its symmetrical beds, the Shamrock Garden with a yew hedge in the shape of an Irish Harp and a bed shaped like a hand full of red begonias to represent The Red Hand of Ulster, and the Spanish Garden framed by a neat arcade of clipped cypress trees.

The gardens also contain a considerable amount of statuary including the famous dodos and ark on the terrace. The statues all relate to the Ark Club – a social circle set up by Lady Londonderry in London during WW1. Each member of the club was given an animal nickname.

The Temple of the Winds is a folly in the classical Greek style built on a high point overlooking the lough. It was designed by James 'Athenian' Stuart in the 1780s.

Super Sun Executive Travel

Twenty

Fiona waited impatiently for Winston to arrive.

"Morning, sweetheart. You extra hungry this morning or didn't you sleep too well last night?'

'Neither. Do sit down, Winston, I've got so much to tell you.'

It didn't take long to update him on the arrival first of Peter Montgomery-Jones and then that of Chester Porter's partner, Allan Trent.

'It was only when Allan said he was his partner that I realised Chester was gay.'

'You din't suspect before?'

'No,' Fiona shook her head. 'Well, I suppose when David Rushworth said his friend was insistent on coming over to take back Chester's body, I did begin to wonder. But not before. I don't think anyone else did either or I would have some inkling of it. It's such a small group. Though I suppose it does explain why he was so reticent to talk much about himself.'

'So what now?'

'I said I'd meet up with Allan after breakfast. He's in a bad way. He'll probably break down completely when he goes to identify the body. He more or less begged me to go with him last night.'

Winston gave her an indulgent grin. 'He ain't your responsibility, sweetheart.'

'I know, but he needs support, and let's face it, there isn't anyone else.'

Fiona was not the only one who wanted to make an early start in order to pass on information. Much to Montgomery-Jones's surprise, his call was answered almost immediately. Andrew Salmon was already at his desk. Either the man had come in at the crack of dawn or he had spent yet another night working right through and had not yet been home.

'Peter. Glad you rang. Something I wanted to tell you. There's been a development.'

'Oh?'

'We've been taking another look at Philip Masterson's background. What seems to have been forgotten in the present investigation is that Philip had a girlfriend, Sally Brent.'

'And that is relevant how?'

'That's the point. Nobody thought it was until now. She didn't make any specific threats against McCollum at the time and didn't appear to have much to do with Edward either, but last Sunday, she left Leeds to go on holiday. She told her family, friends and work colleagues that she was going to some health spa resort in Menorca – one of these yoga and meditation type places. She said she wasn't going to take her phone and they shouldn't to expect to hear from her until she got back. Nobody would have thought anything of it, but for the fact that her father had a stroke a couple of days ago. Not life threatening, but her mother's been trying to get hold of her ever since. The resort denies all knowledge of her and there are no records of her booking a flight or of her arrival at the airport.'

'You are suggesting that she and Edward are in Belfast together?'

'There were two people on that bike. We know Edward has a motorbike licence and – get this – two months ago, Sally Brent joined a gun club. She'd been putting in a lot of time there though she'd told her parents that she'd taken up yoga.'

'Interesting. You think the two of them could be posing as a couple?'

'Exactly. The Belfast police have been busy checking hotel records for single men in Belfast and other towns in the close vicinity, but now we'll have to start again.'

'Is it possible to send me a photograph of her?'

'Ahh. Now there we have a bit of a problem. The most recent one that her mother could provide us with is an old school photo that's twelve years out of date. Apparently, the more recent ones are digital and, as her mother doesn't have a computer of any kind, they are all stored on Sally's laptop which she has taken with her.'

'There must be some on her social media pages.'

'We've been through the lot. Facebook, Twitter, Google +, Pinterest, Instagram, Whatsapp and Viber. It seems, like Masterson, she's closed them all down.'

'But you do have a description?'

'Hang on,' Montgomery-Jones could hear the shuffling of paper as Salmon searched through the papers on his desk. 'Here we are. She's 33 years old, five feet six inches tall, with fair shoulder-length hair.'

'Thank you.' Montgomery-Jones made a note of the details. 'Did you by any chance check on the background details of the other passengers of Chester Porter's tour?'

'No. We had no reason to do so. Did we miss something?'

'Probably not.'

'Anyway, what was it you wanted to tell me?' Salmon sounded more than a little put out.

'I was intending to leave a message. Allan Trent turned up at the hotel late last evening. He was eager to speak to Mrs Mason.'

'He didn't waste much time. I thought he was planning to travel this morning. Have you spoken to him?'

'Briefly. The man was very distressed so there was little point in putting him under any more pressure with a string of questions. However, it is evident that he was Porter's partner.'

'He was gay?'

'It would seem so.'

'Could that be an explanation for why the man was killed? There's a hard core of people who feel very strongly about homosexuals. If he was promiscuous, perhaps he tried to solicit the wrong person.'

'I doubt that. It appears that Porter liked to be discreet about his sexual orientation, which goes someway to explaining the wall of secrecy he appears to have built around himself.'

'If you say so. I take it Trent hasn't spoken to Detective Inspector Flannery either?'

'Not yet. It was gone midnight when we finished talking. I intend to contact the Inspector when he comes on duty.'

'Now the mystery of the dead tourist is cleared up, I suppose you can leave it all with the local police?'

There was a slight pause 'I do not think so. Not just yet. There are still questions to be answered.'

'Yes, but now we know about this girlfriend, it is highly unlikely that Porter is linked to Masterson.'

'Quite possibly but given the lack of success we have had in tracing Masterson; it may be somewhat premature to start closing lines of enquiry. And may I remind you, you were the one who suggested the link in the first place.'

'Well yes,' Salmon agreed reluctantly. 'But you have to admit, Peter. So far it's all proving pretty tenuous.'

'True. But you could say much the same for this whole line of enquiry. Apart from a threat issued at a highly emotional time following a failed trial to convict McCollum for his brother's murder three years ago, we have also to establish a definite link between Masterson and McCollum.'

'Well, it's your call, I suppose. Have you made contact with my informant yet?'

'My flight did not get in until lunch time. I spent what was left of the day at the station discussing the McCollum investigation with Chief Superintendent Dailey and the officer heading up the enquiry team and Chester Porter's murder with the detective Inspector in charge of that investigation.' If Montgomery-Jones was irritated by Salmon's question, it was not evident in his tone.

'Yes. Sorry.'

'I have, however, arranged a meeting with your informant for later today.'

Fiona and Winston were finalising the timings for the day's activities when Peter Montgomery-Jones entered the restaurant.

'Good morning Fiona, Mr Taylor. May I join you?'

'I would be upset if you didn't!' she answered him.

He smiled and took a seat.

'Did you contact Detective Inspector Flannery last night?'

Peter shook his head. 'There was little point by the time we had finished talking. I have left a message for him to ring me this morning.'

'I presume the first thing he will want to do is to take Allan to the mortuary. Allan was in such a state last evening, it's clearly going to be something of a traumatic experience for him. I'd be more than happy to accompany him as he asked. Do you think Detective Inspector Flannery will allow it?'

Peter raised an eyebrow. 'To support Allan or because you want to find out what is going on?'

'Are you accusing me of trying to muscle into your case?'

He gave her an indulgent smile. 'It would not be the first time. You have to admit, Mrs Mason, that you cannot resist a mystery.'

'I think that's probably my cue to leave,' said Winston getting to his feet. 'Now play nice, you two.'

'I'm sorry, Winston.' She had forgotten he was still there.

'Promise me, you two ain't going to come to blows if I'm not here to referee.'

'Oh, I think you know this young lady is more than capable of holding her own in any difference of opinion.'

The two men exchanged conspiratorial smiles, leaving Fiona uncertain as to whether she was amused or felt patronised by the exchange.

Some ten minutes later Allan Trent appeared in the doorway. He looked considerably less harassed than he had done the previous evening.

'I must apologise for my emotional state last night.'

She patted the seat next to her. Once he'd sat down, she asked, 'Not at all. Did you get any sleep?'

He smiled. 'I did. I slept surprisingly well, actually. I think I must have been physically, as well as emotionally, drained.'

'I'm so glad you feel rested, Allan, because I think today is going to prove another tough one.'

'I need to inform Detective Inspector Flannery, who is heading the investigation of Mr Porter's death, that you have arrived. I anticipate that he will wish to speak to you, and I am sure there must be many questions that you would like to ask him,' Peter said.

Allan nodded glumly.

'But for now,' Fiona said brightly, 'As my driver, Winston is always keen to tell me, a good breakfast is essential if you're going to face the day properly. May I recommend you try the fried soda bread? It's an Irish speciality and it's delicious.'

Montgomery-Jones returned to his room. He glanced at his watch and took out his mobile.

'Good morning, James. Anything happening at Vauxhall House that I need to know about?'

'No, sir. A couple of memos came through with dates for future meetings, one with the Anti-Terrorism Policy Committee and a second with the Joint Heads of Staff Government Liaison Group. I've put them in your diary.'

'Good. I would like you to contact the Super Sun Head Office and obtain a list of all the passengers booked on the Belfast tour. Check that all the addresses and the personal details are valid. Plus, if it is at all possible, photo identification of each passenger.'

'Financial details too?'

'No. I simply want to know that each passenger is in fact who they say they are.'

'I see.'

'And James. Make it a priority.'

'Certainly, sir.'

Allan had appeared relatively relaxed as they drove to the mortuary, but Fiona could detect the mounting tension as they sat waiting in a side room while the body was brought up to the observation room.

As one of the staff explained the identification procedure to him, Fiona put her hand on his forearm and gave it a gentle squeeze. 'It won't be that bad, I promise. I had to do it two days ago. He looks very peaceful. They will only uncover his face briefly. Just long enough to give you a chance to recognise him.'

He clapped his free hand over hers and held on tightly as they were led into the small room and over to the covered body on the gurney.

'Can you confirm that this is Chester Porter, Mr Trent?'

Allan nodded.

The whole process was over in seconds and they were led back along a short corridor and shown into another room where Detective Inspector Flannery and Peter Montgomery-Jones were waiting.

'We have some paperwork here that we need to complete with your help, but if you'd like some time to recover first that will not be a problem,' said the Inspector.

'No,' Allan replied in a slightly quavering voice. He continued more firmly, 'I'd rather get it over with, if you don't mind.'

'Firstly, can you give me his full name?'

'It's Lindsey Albert Porter.'

The Inspector looked up sharply. 'Lindsey! I thought he called himself Chester?'

'Chester always hated the name Lindsey. He always said

he was bullied at school because of it. When he went to university, he changed it. He was a great rock music fan. His favourite band at the time was the American group, Linkin Park. Their lead vocalist was a chap called Chester Bennington, which is how he came to choose the name.'

'That explains why the police failed to find any records for a Chester Porter,' Montgomery-Jones said quietly. 'They were not even able to trace his place of work.'

When all the formalities had been completed, Fiona and Allan returned to the hotel, leaving Montgomery-Jones and Detective Inspector Flannery to discuss the progress being made on the investigation.

'Apart from the confirmation that death took place sometime between midday when he was last seen and early evening and that he died from asphyxiation following an upward thrust of a narrow blade between the eighth and ninth thoracic vertebrae, we're not much further forward. We still have no clue as to the who or the why.' Inspector Flannery ran a hand over his balding head.

'If we are agreed that robbery was unlikely to have been the motive, the missing wallet and mobile phone suggests that the killer wished to delay the identification of the victim.'

'Agreed. The location of the body might also suggest that the intention was to delay it being found. Although we can't rule out that it might just be because there was no time to conceal it any better.'

'All of which suggests that the killer may have known the identity of the victim.'

'According to Trent, and from what Porter told his fellow passengers, he had no association with Belfast or Northern Ireland,' said the Inspector. 'Nor, if Trent is to be believed, had he ever shown any interest in what was happening over here. Porter wasn't interested in any kind of politics.'

'It would seem illogical for someone to follow him all the way to Belfast to kill him in a place where there was the possibility of the act being seen. Presumably, it would be so much easier to do on home territory. Which leads to the inevitable conclusion that his killer is likely to be one of his fellow passengers.'

'I think we need to pursue that line of enquiry,' agreed the Inspector.

'May I suggest that you act quickly? The group are scheduled to catch the ferry back to Liverpool tomorrow evening. However, as I understand it, they will check out of the hotel mid-morning.'

Twenty-One

All but one of her passengers were sitting on the coach. Fiona glanced at her watch.

'Does anyone know if Douglas intended coming this afternoon?' When she received no answer, she said, 'We'll give him a few more minutes.'

They couldn't wait much longer, Fiona decided. The coach was only supposed to drop-off and pick-up outside the hotel entrance. Someone would be out to move them on if they stayed much longer.

Fiona was about to go and search for the late arrival when she saw Douglas hurrying across the lobby.

'Sorry, sorry, sorry,' he announced to everyone as he leapt on board. 'No excuse. I just didn't realise the time. I don't know where that last quarter of an hour disappeared to.'

'Not to worry. You're here now. Buckle up everyone and we'll be on our way.'

Fiona felt much more confident as the coach headed east out of the city to the north tip of Strangford Lough. Allan Trent had seemed much more in control when she'd left him so she need feel no more responsibility for him. Time to relax and enjoy the rest of the day.

It was a forty-minute drive to Mount Stewart House, only just over thirty to the lough, so she could not rest for long.

'In a few moments, we'll be reaching the north shore of Strangford Lough which you can see coming into view on the right side of the coach. This beautiful stretch of water is not a lake but an inlet. There is a long narrow channel or strait into the Irish Sea. It's the largest inlet in the British Isles and it contains at least seventy islands. It is also only one of three officially designated Marine Nature Reserves in the United Kingdom. Strangford Lough was designated as Northern Ireland's first Marine Conservation Zone in 2013. In the same year, it was also designated a Special Area of Conservation under the EU Habitats Directive. The road runs right along the coast all the way to Mount Stewart House so keep a look out for the abundant wildlife, which is recognised internationally for its importance. It's a beautiful drive so sit back and enjoy. You won't need me to tell you that Strangford Lough is a popular tourist destination noted for its fishing and scenery.'

As the coach turned off the coast road, through the stone gateway and up the long drive, Fiona picked up the microphone again.

'Once I've bought the tickets, I'm going to lead you to the formal gardens where we are going to meet our volunteer garden guide. She will take us through each of these very different gardens and tell us all about their creation by Edith, Lady Londonderry. After that, you'll be free to look around the house at your leisure. There are several trails in the extensive parklands belonging to the estate. Even if you don't want to do the whole thing, you might like to do the first stretch of the red trail which will take you to the Temple of the Winds. This is a fascinating folly and is one of the finest neo-Classical buildings in Ireland. It's built on one of the highest points on the estate so it's worth going up to the top for the magnificent views. It was built by Robert Stewart, the 1st Marquess of Londonderry who like many wealthy young men of his day, went on the Grand Tour of Europe and inspired by the Greek temples that he saw, commissioned the famous architect of the day James 'Athenian' Stuart to design a folly. Unusually, it's octagonal in shape and is large enough to act as a banqueting hall for holding quite large parties as you will be able to see.'

At two o'clock precisely, Montgomery-Jones crossed the lobby to the front door of the hotel. He had changed into casual slacks and an open-necked, short-sleeved shirt. With a copy of the Insight Guide to Belfast tucked under his arm, he looked every inch a tourist.

The doorman stepped forward. 'May I get you a taxi, sir?'

'I have ordered one already. I am expecting him any minute.'

'Is it for a guided tour of the murals?' Montgomery-Jones nodded. 'He's waiting for you, sir.'

The doorman gave a loud whistle and a black cab appeared from a side street and pulled up in front of the two men.

Montgomery-Jones opened the door, smiled at the driver and said, 'Good afternoon.'

The driver muttered a response. His expression was guarded.

As the taxi headed towards the west of the city, the driver seemed ill at ease. The standard tour was scheduled for an hour and a half so Montgomery-Jones was in no hurry to elicit the information Salmon's informant could give him. His plan that they should take the standard route through the Belfast republican and loyalist areas made famous by the Troubles, was intended to provide cover for them both. To the observer, it would appear that the driver was regaling his passenger with the history and politics of Belfast's notorious period. However, unless he could get the driver to relax and behave more naturally, his plan could be in jeopardy.

'Tell me about the murals. I read that the ones here on the International Wall are regularly changed. Is that correct?'

After a stilted start, the driver went into his spiel and ten minutes or so later, enthused with his subject, he began to smile, and the tension began to ebb away. Time to get down to business.

'London is concerned that you have made no contact in the last few days.'

'I've already told him. I want out. It's too dangerous. After what's happened, the men at the top are jumpy and everyone's under suspicion. Right now, they are all too busy playing power games with each other to worry about me, but any day soon they're going to work out it was me who told you about the arms shipment.'

'Have you thought about the consequences if you attempt to inform them that you are no longer prepared to fight for the cause and intend to leave the group? Do you honestly think there would be no repercussions? If you decide to disappear, even if they fail to track you down – which is doubtful, these are determined men with long memories and unforgiving natures – you will spend the rest of your life looking over your shoulder. You may be able to tolerate that for yourself, but what about your wife and family? You might escape the country, but you will leave your parents, your brothers and sisters and their children behind. Can you guarantee their safety?'

There was a long silence. 'Even if I stay, it don't mean I have to tell you anything more.'

'That is true.'

Montgomery-Jones saw the driver staring at him in the rear-view mirror, eyes wide with surprise.

Montgomery-Jones smiled back. 'What did you expect? That I came to put pressure on you to continue giving us information. What would be the point? If I were to threaten to betray you to McCollum's associates if you failed to continue to co-operate with us, would good would it do? You would never be able to act naturally in front of them in the future. You would betray yourself within weeks. They would smell your fear. Though, from what you have just been saying, that is already starting to happen.'

The taxi slowed to a crawl. The driver gave a long, drawn-out sigh and, in a voice barely above a whisper he said, 'I should never have agreed to start passing on information in the first place.'

After a long silence, Montgomery-Jones said softly, 'Tell me about the early days. Why did you join the CIRA in the first place?'

'It's a long story.'

'We have plenty of time.

'I grew up when Bobby Sands went on hunger strike protesting about the discrimination against Catholics. The whole system was stacked against us. Do you know what he was convicted of? Possession of a revolver! Not murder, not even attempted murder. Just possession. He didn't even have it on him. The police stopped the car and they found a gun so they arrested the driver and all three passengers. The judge sent him down for 14 years. For possession!' He banged a hand on the steering wheel. 'He spent the first 22 days "on boards".
You know what that means? They left him without a stick of furniture in his cell. Then they took away his clothes. He was kept naked for 15 days, and every three days he was given just bread and water. How is that justice? Is that any way to treat a human being? Is it any surprise we grew up angry?'

'Not the best of environments to grow up in, certainly.'

'We all hoped things would be better after the Peace Agreement. The fighting may have stopped, but the injustice goes on. Have you any idea how hard it is to get a decent job for the likes of us in Belfast? You go along for the interview and just when you think it's in the bag, they ask what part of the city you grew up in. As soon as they hear you were born on a Catholic street, they can't get you out the door quick enough. So much for equal opportunity and anti-discrimination policies.' His jaw set in a firm line.

'Point taken.'

'The deaths of the hunger strikers may have hit the world's media at the time, but nothing's changed. That's why I joined the CIRA. To get justice.' His shoulders slumped. 'But that's not what it's about anymore. It's not fighting for a cause; it's just killing for killing's sake. Eamon McCollum wasn't interested in winning justice for working class Catholics. None of them are. Killing the enemy is one thing, but too many innocent people are dying in the process. That business with Philip Masterson was the final straw. The car aimed straight for the back wheel of his bike. I saw his body fly over the handlebars and heard the crunch as his head smashed on the pavement. All those deaths, but that's the one I remember. The one I still have nightmares about.'

There was a long silence.

'What do you think will happen now that McCollum is dead?'

The driver snorted. 'Things will get worse! Patrick Aherne was Eamon's right-hand man, but the old guard were losing their grip long before Eamon was shot. That's what made Eamon more reckless, planning bigger and more spectacular jobs to try and stamp his authority on the dissenters. Show he still had the bottle. As to the future, my money's on John O'Connor. He has a lot of support amongst the younger ones. He's a cold, ruthless bastard. Makes Eamon look like a pussy cat. I wouldn't put it past him to have had a hand in Eamon's death. I'm not saying he'd have been the one to pull the trigger. He's too clever for that, but let's just say, he's shown a great deal of sympathy to Eamon's mother since her son's been in custody. Even been up to the hospital a few times.'

'You think he could have passed on details of McCollum's intended visit?'

'I'm not saying anything. But someone must've. How else would they know when he was going? The details weren't exactly posted on Facebook now were they!'

Twenty-Two

Fiona decided to take a leisurely stroll around the lake. The formal gardens and the house, though far from being crowded, had been busy, but the grounds were so extensive and visitors so spread out that she passed few people as she wandered along admiring the extensive vista of woodland across the large seven-acre lake with its shapes and colours reflected in the water.

The path wound around a wide bend boarded on either side by tall shrubs and trees. The rhododendrons, magnolias and azaleas were long since passed, but the lush greens made the stroll well worthwhile. As she emerged out into the open once again, she spotted Beryl and David resting on a bench.

'Hi there, Fiona.' Beryl waved then moved her bag and shuffled a little closer to her husband to make room for Fiona.

'What a glorious view,' Fiona said as she sat down beside her. 'And the weather couldn't be better, could it?'

'Perfect. I always think that gardens look their best when the sun is shining. The formal gardens were really something. Some of the best we've ever seen, don't you think, pet?' She turned momentarily to David who nodded. 'And each one is so different. I think my favourite was the one with a hedge cut in the shape of an Irish harp, and the flowerbed that looked like a blood-red hand. Though the rose garden was pretty special too. I'm so glad we came.'

'Did you like the house or haven't you been around it yet?'

'Oh yes. Did you notice that chandelier shaped like an old

sailing ship? Wasn't it canny?'

Beryl enthused for the next five minutes making it difficult for Fiona to get away.

'I still haven't been as far as the Temple of the Winds yet and I'd rather like to see it before we leave so if you'll forgive me, I'm going to move on. Enjoy the rest of your afternoon both of you.'

The path around the lake was relatively flat and easy, but it took far longer than the map on the board by the house had suggested. Her frequent stops to take photos or watch the antics of the ducks paddling about at the edge of the water squabbling with each other and chasing away any coots who wandered into their territory every now and again didn't help. Fiona glanced at her watch. The Temple of the Winds was on one of the trails on the far side of the house. It was far too warm to hurry, and in any case, the whole place exuded an atmosphere of peacefulness and calm that it would be a sacrilege to break by undue haste. Nonetheless, if she was going to make it in time she couldn't afford to linger.

Perhaps it was that desire to absorb the quiet serenity of the place that made her notice the two people beyond the little bridge. They were striding quickly through the trees just off the path talking earnestly together completely oblivious of the beauty of their surroundings. They had disappeared before she could be sure, but she could have sworn that the two were Douglas and Stephanie. There was no reason why the two of them should not have been together. As the two remaining single travellers, it was only natural that they should pair up on occasions. Though, given that the group was so small, it was noticeable that when everyone was together, the two seemed to make a point of keeping well away from one another. Even at mealtimes, when it would have been almost inevitable that they should at least sit at the same table, Fiona could not recall a single occasion when they had. Oh well, hers not to reason why. As long as it didn't cause a problem for anyone else, it was hardly her concern.

Some twenty-five minutes after the taxi had delivered Montgomery-Jones back to his hotel, he walked into Chief Superintendent Dailey's office.

'I have just returned from an interesting encounter with Salmon's informant. It took some time to get him to trust me – as Salmon intimated, he is very skittish – but I think we may have some positive leads.'

Once Montgomery-Jones had finished his story, the Chief Superintendent was on the phone issuing orders to his team. There was a satisfied smile on Dailey's face when he eventually ended the call.

'Even if our man did see a Norton Dominator in the old warehouse where the cell regularly meet up, we have no proof that it was John O'Connor who arranged for McCollum to be eliminated,' Montgomery-Jones pointed out.

'True, true.' Dailey's excitement was evident. 'But it does make sense for him to set things up to enable outsiders such as Edward Masterson and Sally Brent to do the actual shooting. That way, if the two were caught, there would be nothing to incriminate him,'

'I agree,' said the normally dour Detective Chief Inspector, catching his superior's enthusiastic mood. 'We may not be able to tie him to it yet, but at least now we know where to look. And, as you say, everything fits. O'Connor is a nasty piece of work. He's been on our radar for some time. Getting rid of McCollum makes perfect sense as far as he's concerned. He can now step in as top dog with little opposition. I'll admit he wasn't at the top of our suspect list at the beginning, but we certainly didn't rule him out. Our problem was that he had an unbreakable alibi for the time McCollum was shot. I agree, using two fanatical outsiders to do the deed means that he could keep his hands clean. We'll never break O'Connor, but if we can find this other couple, we might just get a conviction.'

Fiona passed several of her passengers on the way back past the house. If they thought she was rude simply giving them a wave and a smile and walking on without stopping to chat, so be it. She was determined to see the Temple of the Winds before leaving.

Some distance ahead, she spotted Colin and Louise. They were also going in the direction of the trail so, although she was catching them up, at least it wouldn't be a problem. As she got closer, she realised that the two were arguing. She was too far away to hear what they were saying but the last thing she wanted was for them to think she was spying on them, so she had to slow down and hope they would not stop altogether.

The path up to the temple lay off the main track to the left. Whether Colin and Louise failed to notice the sign, or their plan was to walk the whole of the circular trail leaving out the uphill diversion to the eighteenth-century folly, Fiona had no way of knowing. Whatever the case, she felt a sense of relief when they walked on. It saved any potential awkwardness of meeting up at the temple.

She was out of breath when she reached the crown of the hill. It was by no means a difficult climb, but aware of the time, she had quickened her pace. To give time for her heart to return to normal, she pulled out the guide she'd bought in the shop and read the details about the Temple.

According to the literature, it was possible to hire the building, which could cater for up to 60 guests, as a wedding venue. Inside, she wandered around the edge of the room with its elegant high green walls looking out at the magnificent views from each of its tall windows. A spiral staircase with a wrought iron balcony led up to the top floor. Reaching the top, she stood for some moments admiring the view watching the distant sailboats gliding over the waters of Strangford Lough.

From her vantage on the highest point, she could see people sauntering along the path at the edge of a wide expanse of grass below. She thought she could recognise two of them. Douglas and Stephanie. They were sitting on the grass deep in conversation. There were two or three families eating picnics spread out on blankets. Everyone was enjoying a pleasant summer's afternoon in a beautiful tranquil spot.

She fished into the depths of her bag to find her smartphone to take a photo or two.

A sudden scream made her look up. Two men had emerged from the trees. Dressed from head to toe in black, their faces were covered by balaclavas. One held a machine gun and the other a rifle. A short volley of rapid fire over the heads of the terrified spectators sent them running in panic. The second burst drowned out the screaming.

The other man slowly raised his rifle and took aim.

Douglas scrabbled to his feet. He grabbed Stephanie's arm pulling her to her knees. Suddenly he spun sideways, clutching his upper arm. He took several stumbling steps then ran for cover. He had almost reached the trees when a second bullet caught him in the thigh. He leapt in the air, took two more stumbling steps and fell forward. Motionless.

Stephanie was still on her knees. Suddenly her arms flew high in the air as she recoiled from the impact. In slow motion, her body toppled sideways, a deep red stain slowly spreading over her flowery blouse.

Twenty-Three

Paralysed with shock, Fiona watched as the two gunmen ran down the slope towards the lough disappearing into the trees that obscured the lakeshore. Suddenly, an inflatable dinghy momentarily roared into sight along the shoreline heading inland. It must have stopped just long enough for the gunmen to pile in because a minute later, when it came back into view heading back out into deeper water, three men were clearly visible, the two gunmen still holding their weapons. Even though one of them had removed his balaclava and was looking back at the shore, he was too far away for Fiona to be able to identify him should she ever see him again.

The inflatable did a slow turn and disappeared in the direction it had come.

Fiona raced down the final slope towards the path to be met with utter chaos. People were everywhere, some running away from the waterside, several clutching bleeding limbs and others rushing to see what was happening. Coming towards her was a man struggling to support another with a bleeding leg that he was having trouble putting weight on. Several others also had serious injuries, but she couldn't stop. She had to get to Stephanie.

She had to pass at least two bodies sprawled on the grass that looked beyond help before she reached Stephanie who was now lying collapsed on her side. Her eyes were half closed, and she gave no response when Fiona shouted her name. Blood was pouring from a wound just below her shoulder, but she was still breathing. Just. Fiona pulled her cardigan from her bag and pressed it against the wound and held Stephanie's body tight against her chest.

'You're going to be all right. Help is coming. Keep fighting, Stephanie.'

Fiona was not aware of the passing of time until the man dressed in a dark green uniform knelt in front of her. His eyes looking into hers. He was saying something, but he had to repeat himself several times before the words made sense.

'She's gone, my lovely. Let me take her.'

She heard the words, but somehow, they still didn't register. Her whole body was rigid. Locked. Time stood still.

Then she sensed someone else kneeling down behind her. Arms reached round to take her hands and gently released them from the body to enable the paramedic to take it.

'You can let her go now, Fiona.' A voice she recognised. And the distinctive smell of his aftershave.

Her body went limp and she collapsed back against him. Hot tears welled behind her eyes and she turned, sobbing into his chest as he wrapped her tightly in his arms, murmuring softly into her hair.

She had no idea how long she stayed there locked in his arms. At some point, she vaguely recalled that she was wrapped in a blanket and carried some distance to a car. She must have slept for much of the journey because she only came to at the sound of a low voice over her head saying very quietly, 'Drive us around to the side door. Best not to make an entrance going through the main lobby.'

The car stopped and she opened her eyes. She was lying on his shoulder. His arm still tight around her.

'Hello, sleepyhead.'

'Peter. Where are we?'

'Back at the Hilton.'

Slowly, she levered herself up. Even so, she must have moved too quickly because her head began to swim.

'Take it easy.'

'I'm fine. Just give me a minute.'

The driver, a uniformed police officer, opened her door and helped her out. Peter was by her side before she had a chance to put both feet on the ground. Despite the warmth of the summer evening, Fiona began to shiver and pulled the blanket more closely across her chest.

The driver retrieved her tote bag from the back seat and handed it to Montgomery-Jones.

'Thank you.'

They stood watching as the driver returned to the car and drove off. Once he'd gone, with Peter's help, she took a few tentative steps. By the time, she'd crossed the pavement and reached the door, she felt a little stronger. They must have looked quite a spectacle, and she was grateful that there was no one around to see them either downstairs or as they journeyed up to the fourth floor in the lift. She smiled to herself, she must be feeling better to think such thoughts.

When they reached her room, he took her key from her bag and unlocked her door.

'You will probably feel much better for a shower. Do you think you can manage or would you like help?'

She raised an eyebrow.

He gave a low chuckle. 'You are clearly feeling much better.'

Catching sight of herself in the bathroom mirror was a shock. She knew she was covered in Stephanie's blood, the front of her blouse was sticky with it, but she hadn't realised the extent to which it was still streaked over her forehead and cheeks and her hair was matted with deep crimson strands.

Slowly, she unbuttoned her blouse and dropped it on the floor then removed the rest of her clothes, adding them to the pile. Washing might remove the stains, but she would never be able to bring herself to wear them ever again.

The water ran red when she first stood under the shower. She closed her eyes and lifted her head letting the water tumble over her face and body for some time.

A fleet of ambulances left the scene of the carnage, their blue lights flashing as they headed for the Royal Victoria Hospital in Belfast. Several others carrying those with less serious injuries were dispatched to the Ards Hospital in the nearest town of Newtownards. A small army of paramedics dealt with the myriad of minor cuts and bruises mainly caused in the panic as everyone rushed from the lakeside following the gunfire.

Attempting to bring some sort of order to the chaos, police with loud hailers asked for those who had not been involved in the incident to return to their vehicles in the car park. Although the crowds gradually thinned, there were many anxious people pestering for information about family and friends from whom they had become separated.

Once the emergency vehicles had left, the police and staff marshalling the traffic allowed the cars to leave. The car park was almost empty, and tension was mounting on the Super Sun coach.

'There's still several of us not here.' Irene knelt on her seat looking back to see who was missing. 'Do you think they've been hurt?'

'There's still a lot going on down by the lakeside. The police are taking statements so it might take a while yet. Let's just wait and see.' Winston's reassuring voice exuded his usual calm.'

'But Fiona's not here!' Irene persisted.

'I expect that's because she's trying to find out what's going on.' Winston made his way to the drinks station by the side door. 'This is normally Fiona's job so I ain't as expert at it as she is, but I can make coffee or tea.' He took down the paper cups and looked at them. 'And there's chocolate here too if anyone fancies that. Do I have any takers?'

Before long, everyone had a drink in their hands. It helped keep them busy and for a few moments at least, to take their minds off what might have happened to their missing fellow passengers.

'Four passengers, plus Fiona,' said Beryl as she came back to her seat after collecting up the empty cups.'

'Here's Colin and Louise now,' a voice called out from the back.

The door hissed open and Louise, sporting a large white bandage on her wrist got on first.

'Oh, my goodness, were you shot?' Irene asked.

Louise gave a weak smile and shook her head. 'No. We hadn't reached the clearing when we heard the gunfire. We had no idea what was happening, but when people began bursting through the trees screaming and crying, we ran with them. I managed to fall over in all the rush. My wrist feels pretty sore, but it's not broken or even badly sprained, so the paramedic told me. I was lucky.' She lifted her forearms to reveal grazed elbows. 'These feel a bit raw too.'

'You've got blood on your trousers, pet,' David pointed out.

Louise looked down at the stained ripped material at both her knees. 'I did go a cropper.'

'Do you know what happened to the others?' asked Beryl.

Colin said, 'We saw Fiona going down to the clearing. She's not been hurt, so I suppose she went to help the injured. There are lots of people to see to so I suppose she must still be down there.'

'Did you see Douglas or Stephanie? They still aren't here,' asked Irene.

'We could be a while yet folks, so let's all make ourselves comfy,' said Winston. 'It won't do no good to start speculating. We'll give it ten more minutes and if they still aren't here, I'll go and see if I can find out.'

Twenty-Four

Peter was on his mobile when Fiona finally emerged from the bathroom. He switched it off and turned to her.

'I was beginning to think you had been washed away. How are you feeling now?'

'Much, much better. I'm sorry I went to pieces…'

'No one expects you to be superwoman.'

Pulling the edges of the oversized towelling bathrobe more tightly across her chest, she sank down on the bed. Peter came to sit beside her and sliding an arm around her shoulder, he gently pulled her to him.

'There's blood on your suit!' She hadn't noticed before.

He smiled and shook his head. 'It can be cleaned.'

She laid her head on his shoulder. 'Thank you for looking after me.'

'My pleasure.'

She pulled back and looked into his eyes, 'Shouldn't you be elsewhere. Trying to find the gunmen?'

'Probably.' He made no effort to move.

'Do you know what happened to Douglas? I saw him being shot. He lay on the ground. I thought he was dead at first, but when I got down there, he was gone.'

'You were there?' His eyes narrowed. 'I thought you went down to the scene after it all took place.'

'I did, but I was up at the top of the Temple of the Winds when the shooting started. I saw it all happen.'

'Tell me.'

'Only when you've found out what's happened to

Douglas.'

At first, she thought he might make some excuse, but he must have realised she meant every word. With a sigh, he got to his feet and walked over to the window pulling out his mobile once again. Still feeling incredibly weary, she shuffled to the head of the bed, lifted her legs and collapsed back against the pillows.

She opened her eyes when she heard him walking back and shifted her position so that he could sit on the side of the bed.

'It seems that Mr Redhill is currently in surgery. His injuries are not life-threatening, but he lost a great deal of blood before the paramedics arrived.'

As the realisation struck her, she sat up quickly. Too quickly. Her head began to spin. 'The others! They'll all be wondering where I am. I need to speak to Winston. Was anyone else hurt?'

'I have no information about your other passengers as such, but none of them are on the list of those who died or with serious injuries. We will know more when the coach returns.'

'It's still there?'

'As far as I know. There is a great deal of confusion still so we will have to be patient.'

She grabbed onto his arm. 'Winston! I need to phone him. He'll be worried about me.'

Peter patted her hand, then rose from the bed and retrieved her tote bag from the chair and handed it to her. She tipped out its contents onto her lap and snatched up her mobile.

'Sweetheart!' She could hear the relief in his voice. 'Is you okay?'

'Absolutely fine, Winston. I'm so sorry I've taken so long to ring you. I've been helping with the injured. Where are you? Is everyone okay?'

'We's here in the car park. We's been waiting for you and a couple of the other passengers.'

'I'm afraid Douglas was shot. He's not in any serious danger, but he's been taken to hospital in an ambulance. Stephanie was also shot and… she's been taken away too. So, apart from those two, is anyone else hurt?'

'No. They's all safe and sound and sitting here on the coach. The police won't let us go until they've taken statements from everyone, so it's taking a while.'

'In that case, drive back to the hotel when they let you go, and I'll meet you there.'

'Will do, sweetheart. Take care.'

'You too, Winston.'

She ended the call and caught Peter's expression as she looked up.

'What's that look for?' she demanded.

He held up his hands as though warding off her challenge. 'I was just admiring the way you handled that.'

'I could hardly tell them Stephanie was dead,' she said, her voice beginning to break. 'Besides, I didn't lie.'

'Exactly. The truth, but not the whole truth!'

'I learnt from the master, Mr Montgomery-Jones,' she snapped.

He chuckled. 'They will find out eventually from all the media coverage.'

'True,' she sighed. 'But with any luck, the names of the victims won't be released for some time. Relatives will need to be informed first. And tomorrow, we will all be leaving on the ferry back to Liverpool.'

He raised an eyebrow. 'I would not be too sure of that.'

'Oh? What aren't you telling me?'

'A serious incident has taken place and the police may not be prepared to let you all leave until they have taken statements from everyone who was there. With so many people visiting the house and gardens, that might take some time.'

'Winston said they're doing that now.'

'Initial enquiries maybe. But as more is discovered about the incident, they may have further questions to ask.

Consequently, there is a good chance that the police may require potential witnesses to make themselves available for further questioning.'

'That would be totally impractical as you well know. Yes, I accept that they will need to talk to everyone who was in the vicinity, but as far as I know, apart from Douglas and Stephanie, none of the others were there when the shooting took place. So, what aren't you telling me, Peter?'

He sighed. 'They may still have more questions about the death of Chester Porter.'

'Are you seriously suggesting the police think one of them killed Chester?'

'I am not suggesting anything, Fiona. I simply wanted to warn you of the possibility that your return home might be delayed. I honestly do not know. That is the truth. The whole truth.'

'Talking of truth,' she said, 'why were you at the Mount Stewart estate in the first place? Did you suspect something was going to happen?'

He shook his head, a look of surprise on his face. 'I was in Chief Superintendent Dailey's office when the call came through that there had been a major incident.'

Her eyes narrowed. 'It's a forty-minute drive from Belfast.'

He gave a sheepish grin. 'Not in a police car with blue lights flashing. We were there in just over half that time.'

Unconvinced, she said, 'I'll admit things are a little hazy, but you and the paramedic were there only a few minutes after I got to Stephanie.'

He got up from the chair and came back to join her on the bed again. He gently brushed back the wet hair from her forehead. 'No. The paramedic was part of the rapid response team and he'd been trying to take her body from you for over ten minutes. You were in a state of shock.'

She let him take her in his arms again, yielding into the reassurance of his embrace.

'How many people died?' with her face half buried in his

chest, her voice was muffled.

'I believe there were three at the scene, including Stephanie and there are another half dozen with serious injuries who are on the critical list.'

'But that doesn't make sense.'

'What do you mean?'

'One of those men had a machine gun. Between them, they could have killed twenty, thirty people if they had really wanted to. So, why didn't they?'

'Tell me exactly what happened.'

She described the sudden appearance of the gunmen, the first warning volley and the panic that ensued.

'I saw the man with a rifle slowly raise it to his shoulder. He deliberately shot at Douglas. It caught him on the shoulder, spinning him round, but Douglas kept on running and the gunman fired again. I think it caught him on his leg because I saw Douglas do a sort of hop and skip as he went. The gunman kept firing at him. He was hit several times. He was nearly to the edge of the open ground when I saw him fall. As I said, I thought he was dead. I didn't see him when I got to the lakeside, so I assumed he got away.'

'What about Stephanie? Did you see what happened to her?'

'When the shooting started, she wasn't as quick as Douglas. After Douglas lay on the ground, the man with the rifle turned it on Stephanie. She was on her knees by then, but the bullet went into her chest and she fell sideways. That's where I found her, still lying where she'd fallen.'

Fiona closed her eyes tight shut, but a tear managed to escape. She could feel it running down the side of her nose. She felt a gentle finger wipe it away before it reached her lip.

'You said he deliberately aimed at Douglas and Stephanie?'

She nodded. 'That's the odd thing. Why those two? There were lots of people much closer who would have been much easier targets.'

'Did you see the gunman aim at anyone else?'

Her forehead creased in concentration. 'I don't think so. No. I'm sure not. Everything happened so quickly. The men stepped out from the trees, fired off a few rounds then this small dinghy appeared, and the gunmen turned, ran down to the bank and jumped in as the boat roared away. It was all over in a couple of minutes.'

'Did you notice anything special about the dinghy?'

'It was a black rubber inflatable. The driver – pilot, whatever you call him – sat at the back one hand on the tiller. It was very small. There was barely room for the gunmen to pile in with him.'

He folded her into his arms again and they sat in silence for several minutes, her head resting on his shoulder.

Eventually, he said, 'If you intend to meet your passengers when they get back here, it is probably time you got dressed and dried your hair.'

Reluctantly, she pulled away from him and sat up properly. 'You're right.'

'I need to make a few phone calls.' He looked down at his shirt and the front of his jacket. 'It might also be a good idea to make myself a little more presentable. Will you be all right if I leave you? I will be back in ten minutes.'

'Of course.'

'Sure?'

'Go!'

As the door closed behind him, Fiona swung her legs up onto the bed and cuddled her knees letting her body collapse over.

Perhaps she was not feeling quite as strong as she had tried to make out.

Twenty-Five

Fiona was putting the finishing touches to her makeup by the time Peter returned.

'It wouldn't do to look too pale and wan when I welcome back my passengers.' She glanced at her watch. 'They are going to be here soon, and I haven't done anything about placating the restaurant staff. They are not going to be too happy when we turn up an hour late for dinner. They might even refuse to serve us. They probably need the tables for other guests. It's high season and the hotel is full.'

He smiled. 'Already done. I have had a word with reception, and it is all sorted. Dinner is at eight.'

She reached on tiptoe and kissed his cheek. 'What would I do without you?'

'I sometimes wonder.' He smiled down at her.

'Are you going to join us for dinner?'

He shook his head. 'There are things I need to do. I will come down with you and wait until the coach gets here.'

'Don't you think I'm capable of being left on my own? I presume you are needed back at the police station, which is no doubt, where you should have been for the last couple of hours. I'm hardly likely to break down in the next ten minutes, Peter, so go. I will be absolutely fine.'

He laughed, looked at her for moment or two then walked towards the door.

'Peter.'

He turned back.

'When you return to the hotel, will you tell me what's

happening?'

'I am sure Douglas will pull through…'

She shook her head. 'I have a great many questions that need an answer. I think you owe me that. Please, Peter.'

He sighed. 'I could be very late back.'

'I'll be here.'

Fiona waited by the floor to ceiling window in the lobby, looking out for the white coach. As Winston pulled up by the front doors, she was already standing on the pavement ready for him to open the door.

'Welcome back everyone.' She gave them all the biggest smile she could muster.

Winston was on his feet and she found herself wrapped in a bearhug.

'We was all worried about you, sweetheart.'

His words were drowned out by the cacophony of shouts and clapping from behind.

'I am so sorry I gave you all such a fright. I should have phoned Winston much earlier to let you know I was safe, but as you can imagine it was chaos out there. As you can all see, I am absolutely fine. Were any of you folk hurt at all?'

'How are Douglas and Stephanie?' Beryl want to know.

'As to that, I have no more information than I gave to Winston when I phoned earlier, but I promise to let you all know as soon as I hear anything further. Now, it is getting late, but the restaurant has very kindly agreed that they will serve dinner for everyone at eight. So please,' she glanced at her watch, 'you have only seven minutes to get to your rooms, tidy yourselves up and be back down in the restaurant. No more questions for now. Let's go, everyone.'

She helped the last person down the coach steps and watched them disappear towards the hotel doors.

'Winston, I really can't thank you enough for looking after everyone.'

His usual smiling face still looked serious.

'Is you sure you're all right, sweetheart?'

'Absolutely. It's all go at the moment, but we'll get together at breakfast and I'll tell you everything that's been happening. It's been quite an afternoon.'

'As long as you is safe. That's all that matters, sweetheart.'

The police station was buzzing when Montgomery-Jones walked in. Chief Superintendent Dailey was in the incident room deep in discussion with one of his DCIs. He looked up and saw Montgomery-Jones standing in the doorway and came over immediately.

'Just getting an update. Come along to my office. We can talk in there.'

The Chief Superintendent led the way along the corridor and into his outer office pausing briefly at his secretary's desk.

'Do you think you could rustle up some coffee for us please, Janice?'

To Montgomery-Jones, he said, 'I don't suppose you've eaten since lunch, have you?'

'No, but please do not concern yourself on my account.'

'Neither have I,' came the heartfelt reply. 'And it could be a long night.'

'I'll see what I can do, sir.' The matronly woman gave her boss an indulgent smile and picked up the phone.

'You're a treasure.'

As soon as they sat down in the Chief Superintendent's office, the two men got down to business.

'Thanks for the call earlier.'

'I take it you are no nearer to catching the gunmen?' Montgomery-Jones inquired.

'Unfortunately, no. They appear to have disappeared off the face of the earth. We've had boats scouring the shoreline for the last three hours, but Strangford Lough is a damned great stretch of water. It's twenty miles long and the shoreline is full of creeks, bays, coves and mudflats. Literally hundreds of secluded spots where they could have moored up and hidden away the inflatable. It's even conceivable that they went through the mouth of the channel and out into the Irish Sea.'

'It looks as though the getaway was well planned.'

'Too right. In and out before anyone had a chance to draw breath.'

'Has anyone claimed responsibility?'

Chief Superintendent Dailey shook his head. 'It could be the old guard at the CIRA. Revenge for what happened to Eamon McCollum. Though I have to admit, that idea would make more sense if there had been some sort of declaration with it. Something in my water tells me the two events are connected.'

'I agree.'

There was a knock on the door and Janice came in with a tray of coffee and two plates piled high with cottage pie and vegetables.

'I'm afraid that's all that was left in the canteen, sir.'

'It smells magnificent, thank you.'

There was silence for a minute or two as both men tucked into their meal with gusto. The great mound of mashed potato covered in thick brown gravy may not have looked particularly appetising, but there was little left on the plates when the two men had finished.

'We're still going through all the statements that were taken at the scene, which reminds me, how much credence do you give to the evidence the tour manager gave?'

'Mrs Mason has my total confidence. Why? Does it conflict with what has been said by the other eyewitnesses?'

'No, no! Though half of them swear categorically that there were at least half a dozen gunmen and there doesn't seem to be any consensus as to how long the whole thing went on.'

'As is common in such incidents. People panic and were running for their lives. They recall their emotions, what they felt was happening, rather than the actuality.'

'Exactly. That's what I'm saying.'

'Mrs Mason was not running away. She had a high vantage point at the top of the tower well away from the action itself. Her life was not in danger.'

'True. But you yourself said she was suffering from extreme shock.'

'That was as a result of having someone, for whom she felt personally responsible, die in her arms. That occurred several minutes after the shooting and the men had disappeared.'

'I don't query her statement about that or that there were two gunmen, but your Mrs Mason was the only one who noticed the inflatable.'

'Even if the other witnesses were not running away, the convex slope and the trees between the clearing and the water's edge would have prevented anyone seeing it from below. Mrs Mason was at the top of the folly. Even she did not see the gunmen get into the inflatable. It was only visible when it pulled back into deeper water.'

'The trouble is, Peter, that the estate is enclosed by a low wall and the A20 Greyabbey-Portaferry road runs between it and the lough shore. I suppose they could have vaulted the wall easily enough, but there was a risk they'd been seen by passing traffic.'

'So not impossible? Perhaps that's why one of them had removed his balaclava. To check the coast was clear before they left the cover of the trees.'

'Possibly,' the superintendent still sounded sceptical. 'There is another thing. When you phoned, you mentioned that she's adamant that the man with the rifle did not pick his victims at random. That he deliberately selected these two passengers of hers. Isn't it more logical to assume, in order to make a kill, he would take a careful aim and they just happened to be in the line of fire?'

'I take your point. But she claims there were far closer and easier targets that the gunman could have lined up in his sights, but he did not attempt to fire at anyone else. I appreciate, it is much too soon to have anything back from the coroner, but it will be interesting to see if the two others who died were killed by rifle shot or machinegun fire.'

'But Redhill is still alive.'

'Maybe. However, he lay motionless prone on the ground. At the time, Mrs Mason thought he was dead and so presumably, did the gunman.'

'But why those two individuals? What's special about them?'

'That is the question she asked.'

'Any ideas?'

Montgomery-Jones shook his head. 'She also raised another interesting point. When she heard how few people were dead or seriously injured, she was surprised that there were not many more victims. It could have been a massacre, but most of the machinegun fire was above the heads of the crowd. Was that merely a distraction to mask the deliberate killing of specific individuals?'

'A valid point. If this was a terrorist attack intended to make a political point, it was a pretty half-hearted attempt.'

'Presumably the names of the three victims will not be released until next-of-kin have been informed, but may I suggest that for the time being, they are not given to the media until a detailed background check has been made of all the victims, including those who have been seriously injured.'

'I agree. Consider it done. Meanwhile, I think we need a detailed statement from your Mrs Mason as soon as possible.'

'Do you intend to do that now?'

'Is there any reason why not? Do you think she's still in a state of shock?'

Montgomery-Jones gave a slow smile. 'She is probably recovered sufficiently to answer your questions, but by now, she will be fully occupied looking after her charges and I doubt she would react favourably if you attempt to call her away from her responsibilities. Given that I am convinced you will learn nothing more than I have passed on already,

I think you might get a better response if you waited until the morning.'

'Hmm. DI Flannery did mention she could be very fierce.'

'I prefer to think of it as spirited.'

'The morning it is then.'

Twenty-Six

The tables set aside for them in the restaurant were not their usual ones by the windows but in a much darker corner at the side of the room right next to the kitchen doors. Not that any of her passengers showed any concern about their less congenial surroundings or complained that they no longer had the magnificent views of the waterfront. With three of the original party now missing, the group was reduced to four couples. While she was waiting for everyone to arrive, Fiona asked the staff to rearrange the tables so that everyone could sit together. Although none of them had been present at the scene of the shooting, they were all badly shaken and in Fiona's judgement, would find reassurance in the company. Plus, she could help control the worst excesses of wild rumour and misinformed gossip that often followed such traumatic incidents.

For once, Irene and Norman were not the first to arrive.

'My goodness, you look as though you've been in the wars. What happened?'

Louise explained the reason for her bandaged wrist.

'I know I really shouldn't cover them,' she said, raising her forearms to show off the two enormous sticking-plasters in front of her elbows. 'The ambulance man said to leave the raw skin to dry off in the air so that the grazes would scab over more quickly, but the trouble is they catch on everything. I had to change out of what I'd been wearing. My clothes got filthy when I fell, and I ripped one of my favourite blouses. I did try to be careful, but it's impossible to get dressed and undressed without rubbing against the material. My right knee is even worse than my elbows, but I've left the grazes on my shins. I'm just hoping the blood doesn't seep through and stick to my skirt.'

The others started to arrive, and it wasn't long before everyone was asking after Douglas and Stephanie.

'I think it will be a while before we get any more news,' Fiona said, firmly. 'As a matter of fact, I was wondering if I should contact their families and let them know what's happened. Did either of them happen to mention any family earlier by any chance?'

'Douglas isn't exactly the talkative type,' said Colin.

'He did say something about his brother, I seem to remember,' said Beryl. 'We were talking about our last holiday to Norway to see the Northern Lights and I remember he said it was something he'd wanted to do ever since his brother had raved about them. Do you remember, David?'

Her husband gave a frown. 'Can't say I do, pet. Sorry.'

'Oh you! I know I'm right.' Beryl insisted.

'But I do remember Stephanie saying that she worked in a hospital,' David said quickly in a vain effort to retrieve his failings. 'She was a nurse.'

'No. She was a physiotherapist,' Beryl corrected.

'Not to worry.' Fiona decided it was time to step in before the couple came to blows. 'I expect the hospital will sort it out. They have whole systems in place for discovering next of kin in such circumstances.'

Fiona glanced around the table. Irene's face was creased in thought; her lips pinched together. 'Is something the matter, Irene?'

'Don't get me wrong, I hope she gets better soon, but in my opinion Stephanie's not a very nice person. She was very rude to me that day outside the city hall.'

'She can be very offhand and forceful in her views,' Fiona said, 'but I don't think she meant to upset you.'

'Hmm. I'm sure it's part of your job to see the best in

everyone, Fiona, but I'm with Irene on this one,' said Joan Fletcher. 'You should have seen the way she laid into poor Chester that time. She was having a right go!'

'Really? Do you have any idea what they were arguing about?'

'They weren't arguing. Chester just stood there while she read him the riot act about something. I've no idea what. They were too far away for me to hear, but it looked as though she was threatening him.'

'Can you remember when that was?'

'It must have been sometime that day he went missing. But I don't remember exactly.'

Before Fiona could ask any more questions, her mobile started to ring.

'Excuse me everyone, I'll take this outside where I won't disturb you all.'

She hurried out of the restaurant hoping that the caller wouldn't give up before she got outside the doors.

'Hello.'

'I apologise for disturbing you at this late hour, Mrs Mason. This is DI Flannery.'

'Detective Inspector. How can I help?'

'I need to speak to each of your party. I was planning on doing so this evening when you all returned to the hotel, but of course the events of this afternoon made that impractical. I think your passengers have had more than enough drama for one day, so I intend to postpone the interviews until first thing tomorrow morning. My officers will be at the hotel at eight thirty. I would be very grateful if you would inform your party.'

'I see. Thank you for your consideration.'

She had to give the man his due. Even though it was evident that they had no choice in the matter, he had tried to make it sound like a polite request. And he'd been thoughtful enough to delay proceedings so as not to cause more upset for the time being. All the excitement of the afternoon meant that she had given little thought to Chester

Porter. She would return home a great deal more at ease if the mystery of his death could be resolved. Not knowing who committed the crime or why would haunt her for months to come.

Had the police really made so little progress on the case? And why was Peter so interested in it? He was supposed to be in Belfast because of the shooting of the CIRA terrorist Eamon McCollum. Just how much was he keeping from her? Quite why she now felt certain that the two cases were connected, she couldn't explain. Could Chester have been some undercover man and Allan Trent's account of their relationship merely a diversion to stop any further investigation? He had appeared late in the day. Time enough to fabricate some story that might fit the facts. Were either of them who they said they were? And what of today's massacre; how did that fit in? The jigsaw picture was beginning to take shape, but she was missing some vital pieces.

Fiona shook her head. She hadn't the time to dwell on such thoughts now. She had to get back to her passengers and tell them the unwelcome news. With only eight people, she could only hope that the process would not take too long and that interviews would be over long before they were due to leave for Castle Ward and the Game of Thrones tour.

Twenty-Seven

There was a gentle tap on her door. Fiona was out of bed and across the room so quickly that Peter barely had time to lower his hand before she'd flung open the door.

'I saw the light under your door. I just wanted to check that you were all right.'

'I'm perfectly fine, Peter. Come in.'

'You have not been waiting up just for me to return, have you?'

She shook her head and climbed back into bed pulling up the duvet to her chin as she sat propped up on the pillows. 'No, I couldn't sleep. Too much on my mind.'

His brow creased in a worried frown as he stood studying her face. 'You are not still...'

'I've told you, I'm fine. That's not what I meant. I'm just trying to make sense of it all. So how is the investigation going? I appreciate you can't tell me the details and I'm not trying to inveigle them out of you. I just want to know if there's been any progress.'

He gave a long sigh and came to perch on the side of her bed. 'Not really. I passed on what you told me about the gunmen to the officers in charge and the investigating team will send someone to take a formal statement from you tomorrow morning.'

'Another fun day lined up for us then,' she said with a grimace. 'DI Flannery is sending officers to interview my lot about Chester's murder. Before you know it, he'll arrest a couple more of them. At this rate, I'll be going back to

England on my own.'

Peter burst out laughing. It was so rare to see him express such unguarded display of emotion that it took her completely by surprise. In response, she found herself grinning.

Slowly, he leant forward and kissed her softly full on the lips. It was all she could do to stop herself from wrapping her arms around him and pulling him closer.

He pulled back just enough so that he could look into her eyes, but he was still leaning forward, his weight on his arms, his hands one each side of her hips.

'I know exactly what you're up to, Mr Montgomery-Jones. And let me tell you, it isn't going to work.'

'Is it not?'

'Assuredly not! If you think that little diversionary tactic is going to stop me asking probing questions, think again Mr Montgomery-Jones.'

'What a pity.' His eyes continued to twinkle.

She put a hand on his chest. 'Seriously, Peter. There's something I want to ask. Do you know if our mystery man, Chester Porter, really was who he said he was?'

'His friend identified him.'

'Eventually. And don't you think Allan Trent is too...' she searched for an appropriate word, 'OTT to be true?'

'I confess that first evening, I wondered the same thing myself. However, I do not think you need to lose any sleep over the pair of them. According to the human resources manager at Brindle Brothers Ltd., both names are on their list of employees and Porter is down as currently on holiday and Trent on compassionate leave. And talking of sleep, I think it is high time you snuggled down and tried to get some.'

He pushed himself upright again and was about to get to his feet when she put out a hand to hold him back.

'Before you go, there's something I wanted to tell you. It's about Stephanie.'

Instantly the familiar inscrutable Montgomery-Jones was

back. 'What about Stephanie?'

'It may be nothing, but as soon as I got into bed this evening, this picture of her on the day Chester went missing suddenly popped into my mind and I haven't been able to get it out ever since.'

'Tell me.'

'It was when we were by the Palm House waiting for everyone to return. Stephanie tended to wear these long floaty chiffon scarves wrapped round her neck, but she wasn't wearing one when she got back.'

'Perhaps she had decided not to wear one on that day.' Not surprisingly, Peter didn't sound convinced.

'But that's the point, she had. Before we all left to go our own ways before lunch, she got her scarf caught in the teeth of the zip on her bag. I helped her sort it out. But a couple of hours later, when she got back, she no longer had it. I remember distinctly because we were stood around for some time waiting for Chester to return and I noticed the raised mole on Stephanie's neck. It's on the top of her collarbone just here,' Fiona touched the base of her own throat to demonstrate. 'I think that's the reason for the scarves. To cover it up. It's quite prominent, an irregular oval shape and I remember wondering if she'd ever had it checked. Dark moles like that can turn out to be cancerous. The point is, Peter, I have no idea why, but I can't get rid of this feeling that that missing scarf is important. That it's connected with Chester's disappearance that day.'

Peter's face remained impassive. Even if he thought she was rambling and still suffering from some kind of delayed shock, he would never show it in his expression, but somehow, because of the way his eyes were locked on hers, she knew she must be on to something.

'Peter, I know it's asking you to break every rule in the book, but please, tell me exactly how Chester died. I know he was stabbed in the back, but is that what actually killed him, or was it something else?'

For what seemed a long time, he sat in silence staring at

her. 'You are correct. It would break every rule in the book to reveal the details. Let me ask you a few questions first. What makes you think he did not die from the stab wound?'

'Stabbing someone to death in the back is an almost impossible feat. You would naturally hold the knife so.' She held a fist high as through grasping a knife then made with a sudden downward slash. 'Which means that the blade is at the wrong angle. It would simply bounce back against the ribs. To get the blade between the ribs, you would need to hold it like this.' She lifted her elbow high to the side and thrust her hand towards him. 'Even then, you would need medical knowledge to penetrate exactly the right spot to hit the heart to do the most damage. Plus, of course, even if you did manage to find the sweet spot, it would take too long.'

'Meaning?'

'He might bleed to death if he was left for long enough, but I'm assuming Chester was killed not far from the botanic gardens, if not actually in them. A very public area. The killer would need to be quick first to stop him or herself from getting caught and also to ensure that the victim had no time to call for help. So, am I right in thinking Chester did not die from a stab wound?'

He gave an almost imperceptible nod.

'Was he strangled?'

'No.'

Her shoulders drooped. 'Damn! I was so sure I was right.'

'You think it was Stephanie because of the missing scarf?'

'It seemed like a possibility. Plus, the other thing.'

'What other thing?'

'Are you certain Chester was stabbed with a knife?

'Meaning?'

'When Detective Inspector Flannery said he wanted to interview my passengers again tomorrow morning, I thought that meant that one of them must be a suspect. I suppose it was going round at the back of my mind and when I got into bed, I started thinking and I had this vision of Stephanie coming up behind Chester. She's hardly likely to have had a knife in her bag but she might have had something sharp and pointy like a nail file for instance. I learnt this evening that she was a physio so she would have had enough medical knowledge to be able to stab him in the right place. Once he was on the ground and helpless, she could have wrapped the scarf around his neck and pulled it tight. It probably happened so quickly that there was no time for him to call out.' She slumped back against the pillows. 'I was so convinced by my own fantasy, that I got carried away.'

Peter was silent for a long time. He was clearly weighing up something.

'If he didn't die from the stabbing and he wasn't strangled, how did he die?'

The silence went on for what seemed an age but was probably less than a few seconds. 'Your idea does have some credibility. Chester Porter may not have died from strangling, but he was asphyxiated. Something, possibly even the long end of a long floaty scarf, as you put it, was held over his nose and mouth. However, there is a major problem. It does not explain why Stephanie Jessen might wish to kill Chester Porter in the first place. As far as we can tell, the two were complete strangers before the start of the tour and there is nothing to suggest that they have anything in common.'

Fiona let out a long sigh. 'I'm well aware of that. I've been wracking my brains for the last half hour trying to come up with an answer. Joan Fletcher saw the two of them arguing or rather she saw Stephanie berating Chester about something. Now here, I really do appreciate that I'm going out on a limb, but could it be that Chester saw or overheard something he shouldn't?'

'I appreciate that an individual might be irate at a stranger listening in to their private business but killing him for it does seem a somewhat extreme response.'

She glared at him. 'Have you any idea how pompous that

sounds?'

He smiled. 'Enough to provoke you to murder?'

'Point taken. Stop trying to put me off my train of thought.' She chewed on her bottom lip for a moment or two. 'What if, whatever he saw or heard was serious enough for him to threaten to report it to the police? That would explain why she had to act so quickly.'

'The next obvious question is what could Stephanie Jessen say or do that was serious enough for Chester Porter to consider reporting her to the police?'

'Isn't that your job to find out, Peter? You're SIS. You tell me!'

'That might prove somewhat difficult as both parties are now dead.'

'Okay, so let's try this one. You are here in Belfast because a terrorist, supposedly in police custody, was murdered. So, let's put the two things together. What if Chester overheard Stephanie plotting McCollum's murder?' She shook her head. 'No. That won't work. Why would she want to kill McCollum in the first place? Unless she was a committed loyalist, which is hardly likely. So, could Chester have seen her talking with terrorists? But how would he know they were terrorists?'

She looked at Peter. He was wearing his usual inscrutable expression, which meant she had no idea what he was thinking.

Eventually, she broke the silence. 'I'm sorry, Peter. I've just been wasting your time with a load of crackpot theories.'

'Oh no, Mrs Mason. Not at all.' He leant forward and kissed her firmly on the lips. 'You, my dear Fiona, have just cracked the case. I have to go.' He gave her another quick kiss and was gone.

The last kiss may not have had quite the passion that the first had revealed, but the memory of them was enough to make her cuddle down beneath the covers with a warm glow permeating every cell in her body.

Day 8 Sunday

Sadly, this is our last day in Belfast. This morning is the final opportunity for some last-minute shopping before our late start to Castle Ward and our Game of Thrones Experience. Fans of the hit television series will not want to miss this fascinating tour, which will take us to several of the locations used in the series.

We journey to Castle Ward south of Strangford Lough to this magnificent National Trust property, which was transformed to depict the home of House Stark: Winterfell. Our tour begins in the farmyard of the estate, which is where Bran Stark's archery scene in the very first episode was shot. Here we will learn something of the medieval art of archery and have a chance to try out our own skills. That will be followed by looking at some big screen clips of the many special effects that were used during filming including the use of green screens.

Lunch will be served in the restaurant of the 18th-century mansion after which we will be driven down to the lakeside and the Old Castle Ward, built around 1590. For the Game of Thrones, the castle towers were transformed into Winterfell, where the head of House Stark rules over his people. Before leaving these film locations, we will have an opportunity to dress up in actual costumes from the series and have photographs taken to bring back as a memento.

To end this memorable holiday, we will have dinner at a local venue for a true Irish Night. As we dine on sumptuous Irish fare, an award-winning troupe will entertain us with traditional Irish dancing together with local singer-musicians well-known throughout Northern Ireland.

From there, our coach will drive us to the ferry in time to catch the overnight crossing back to Liverpool.

Here at Super Sun Executive Travel we wish you a fond farewell. We hope you enjoyed the "Beautiful Belfast and Northern Ireland" tour and look forward to seeing you all again in the near future.

Super Sun Executive Travel
Specialists in Luxury Short Breaks and
Continental Tours

Twenty-Eight

PC Kennedy shifted uneasily on the uncomfortable wooden chair and gave a deep sigh. His buttocks were complaining bitterly. If he was honest, at his level, the majority of police work was pretty boring. He didn't mind night shift as such, but these watch-and-wait duties were the worst of all. It didn't help that he couldn't stand hospitals. That bing-bong ring in the background every now and again drove him crazy. Heaven knows what it was for.

The room was dark so he couldn't even read the paper. Through the open door, he could see along the corridor to the light above the nurses' station. He could hear the constant murmur of their chatter. He was tempted to go and join them, but if word got back to the sergeant, he'd be disciplined at best and might even be for the chop. Not worth the risk. The nurses brought him cups of tea every now and again. If that pretty redhead came next time, he might be able to get her to stop and talk for a bit.

He stood up, stretched both arms to the ceiling and leaning back, let his mouth fall open in a great yawn.

There was a movement in the bed. The man was restless, he was beginning to wake. He twisted his head fretfully from side to side muttering something.

PC Kennedy hurried to the bedside trying to make out what the man was saying.

'That bloody man... he set us up... the bastard set us up.'

'Who set you up?'

The squirming and the moaning continued, but the sick

man said nothing more that was coherent. He was becoming so agitated he was in danger of pulling out the tubes pumping liquid into his arms.

'Nurse, nurse!'

The policeman leant across the bed and pressed the red call button, but he could already hear the rush of feet in the corridor. He still had his finger on the button, when two nurses came in the door. He was firmly pushed aside before he had a chance to step back.

He made his way out of the room and along the corridor to the window to make his call. The sky was red with the rising sun. It must be later than he realised.

'Can you let the boss know, Redhill's coming round? Tell him, I'll let him know as soon as they say Redhill's fit for questioning. Don't know if it's relevant or not, but he was muttering to himself, something about being set up.' He repeated the exact words the injured man had said and waited for them to be repeated back to him before ringing off.

For once, Fiona woke on the alarm. She'd had a surprisingly good night. She must have fallen asleep straight after Peter had left. With her mind in overdrive, it was amazing that she'd managed to get to sleep at all.

She stretched out an arm and switched off the insistent blare, but instead of leaping straight out of bed, as was her wont, she lay back and let her thoughts roam back over the previous day's events. It was certainly a day she wouldn't forget in a hurry. And not just because of the horrific terrorist outrage on the shores of Strangford Lough.

She could still feel that gentle pressure on her lips and savour the taste of that kiss. Even now, the memory of it produced that same fluttering in the pit of her stomach that it had caused last night.

Telling herself sharply that she was a middle-aged woman – a grandmother to boot – and not some giddy teenager, she threw back the covers and swung her feet to the floor. Time to get back to reality. Besides, logic told her that any kind of relationship was totally out of the question. She and Peter Montgomery-Jones belonged to different worlds. His was a life wrapped up with terrorists, political shenanigans, spies and subterfuge and it was impossible to imagine him by her side in any of the social circles she frequented.

And what of her two boys? It didn't bear thinking about how they might react to a new man in her life. Martin might not approve of his mother showing an interest in another man so soon after his father's death, but he was unlikely to make a great fuss. However, the same could not be said for his older brother. Adam would never forgive her. It was bad enough that he was still trying to persuade her to give up work and take life easy. He just couldn't understand she wasn't ready to spend her days knitting and watching daytime TV. Peter, on the other hand, knew just how important the job was to her. How the bungalow in Guildford had become a virtual prison in those final years before Bill died. At least with Martin based in Edinburgh and jet setting all over Europe and the Near East for his work and Adam settled in Canada with his wife and two small children, she had managed to keep from them all the dangers she'd encountered on her travels. Though most tours involved nothing more stressful than delayed ferries, missing luggage and problem hotel bookings, her life had been threatened on more than one occasion. Introducing Peter Montgomery-Jones as the man who had rescued her from certain death would hardly prove the best of starts. Explaining his presence in her life would be tricky enough. She could hardly tell them he was a member of Her Majesty's Secret Intelligence Service. A civil servant perhaps, but then how could she account for them meeting in the first place?

This was getting her nowhere. Idle fancy. Time for her shower. If she didn't get a move on, she'd be late for her morning meeting with Winston. She had so much to tell him today. She wasn't sure if Detective Inspector Flannery's team would want to interview Winston as well as all her passengers, but she should warn him of the possibility. The Inspector had said he and his team would be arriving at the hotel immediately after breakfast. She would have to keep her fingers crossed that the police wouldn't keep them all hanging around too long. They were due to leave for Castle Ward at eleven o'clock and everyone would need to have checked out of the hotel and have their main cases stowed away under the coach by then.

Of the three men sitting around the table in Chief Superintendent Dailey's office, only Detective Inspector Flannery looked as though he'd had any sleep the night before.

'More coffee, anyone?' Flannery asked, holding the pot aloft.

Montgomery Jones shook his head and the Superintendent muttered, 'If I have any more caffeine, I'll be hyper for the rest of the day.' He pushed away the plate with its half-eaten sandwich which had been sitting on the papers in front of him and leant forward folding his arms on the table looking down at the notes.

'On second thoughts, it's the only thing keeping me awake!' The Chief Superintendent pushed his mug across the table. 'So, do we accept Mrs Mason's assertion that Douglas Redhill and Stephanie Jessen were deliberately targeted by these gunmen yesterday?'

'I'm happy to go with it for the time being until further evidence suggests otherwise,' Detective Inspector Flannery replied, but it was evident from his tone that he had a degree of reservation. 'Although the post-mortems have yet to be carried out, the initial reports confirm that two .40 calibre bullets were recovered from Stephanie Jessen's body, the same calibre as those removed from Douglas Redhill's shoulder and thigh. One of the other victims, a German tourist from Munich, died from .40 calibre bullet wounds consistent with those from a machine gun blast. The other fatality died of a heart attack.'

'So, what do we know about Stephanie Jessen and Douglas Redhill?' asked the Chief Superintendent.

'My department has been looking into the backgrounds of all the members of the Super Sun party, but I have not yet had a full report. I am hoping to receive details later this morning,' Montgomery-Jones said.

'Could this couple be the brother and girlfriend of the witness McCollum is believed to have had run down?' Dailey suggested.

'Edward Masterson and Sally Brent? Possibly, but as yet, we have no evidence to support that theory.'

'But you're convinced that Masterson and Brent are part of the Super Sun party?'

'Convinced, no. Highly suspect, yes. Although I have to admit, I did have another couple in mind entirely. The description of Sally Brent fits Louise Davenport. Right age, build and hair colour. Her husband, Colin is a more difficult match as any pictures we have of Masterson, as you are all aware, show him with a full beard.'

'But I thought Stephanie Jessen had brown hair?' said the Inspector.

'Which she could easily have dyed,' Montgomery-Jones pointed out. 'Although, making the assumption for the time being, that Stephanie Jessen and Sally Brent are one and the same person, it does add credence to Mrs Mason's idea that she was responsible for the death of Chester Porter.'

'Which reminds me, we will need to take a written statement from her ASAP about what she saw at the Mount Stewart estate.' Chief Superintendent Dailey turned to Flannery. 'As you and your team will be going to the hotel to interview all the Super Sun passengers in connection with the death of Chester Porter in an hour or so, you can take a statement from Mrs Mason then.'

'If you say so, sir.'

'You don't look happy, Flannery. Something troubling you?'

'I'm prepared to accept what Mrs Mason says about what happened at the loughside, but I confess I'm a great deal more sceptical about her theory of Stephanie Jessen being responsible for Chester Porter's murder. I appreciate she claims it's pure speculation, based on a missing scarf, but it all seems too fanciful to me. The woman could have lost it anywhere or, more likely, decided that she was too hot so took it off and stuffed it in her bag.'

'Come on, another death in the group has to be suspicious. Two murders and a massacre all within four days! They have to be connected.' Chief Superintendent Dailey was adamant. 'We work on the assumption that the cases are linked – that Stephanie Jessen killed Porter and she and Douglas Redhill became targets themselves. Although we have no evidence to explain why as yet, it's a safe bet that both murders are related to the shooting of Eamon McCollum outside the hospital. Let's go look for evidence, gentlemen.'

Inspector Flannery continued to frown. 'My men did a thorough search of the area around where the body was found. I appreciate that it was a couple of days after he went missing, but the bins hadn't been emptied in the meantime and even they were searched. I admit they weren't specifically looking for a scarf or a nail-file but given that both are likely to have had blood on them, they would have been discovered.'

'Has her hotel room been searched?' asked Montgomery-Jones.

Flannery sighed. 'Not yet. I'll see to it.'

'Make sure they also search Redhill's room, while they're at it,' Chief Superintendent Dailey ordered.

'Yes, sir.'

'And tell your men,' continued Dailey, 'they are looking for anything that might identify them as Masterson and Brent plus anything that might pin either of them to the shooting of McCollum.' He picked up another bacon sandwich from the plate in the centre of the table and took a large bite.

'Let us hope we learn more when Douglas Redhill is questioned,' Montgomery-Jones said. 'If there are no objections, I would like to be present when Redhill is questioned.'

'I see no problem with that. You were the one who suggested that there might be a link between McCollum's shooting, Philip Masterson's brother and this coach party in the first place,' said Dailey. 'Right, thank you, gentlemen,' Dailey shuffled together the papers in front of him and put them back into a manila folder. 'If there is nothing else, let's get to work.'

Fiona rarely bothered to watch television on any of her tours, but it made sense to listen to the news about yesterday's events before facing any of her passengers. She was almost dressed and ready to go down when the report came through. It only lasted two minutes at most. Just that an incident had taken place at Mount Stewart House, that the police and ambulances were called to the estate but no mention of any fatalities. The police appeared to be doing a good job of keeping the details under wraps. It was only as she switched off the TV, she realised she hadn't yet spoken to Head Office.

She seized up her mobile and then paused. Perhaps Winston had already done so. Either way, her call could wait five more minutes until she'd spoken to her driver.

Twenty-Nine

Long after Winston had left to put the main cases into the luggage section of the coach, Fiona sat sipping tea. It was no surprise that Peter Montgomery-Jones had not appeared for breakfast. Most likely, he was already at the police station busy with the investigation. She wasn't sure if she was relieved or disappointed. She hadn't yet worked out how best she should react at their next meeting. It would be foolish to read too much into that kiss. The most mature thing to do would be not to ignore it, pretend it hadn't happened, but to carry on as though it was of no real consequence. Just a show of affection between friends. It need not be an embarrassing encounter, she tried to reassure herself. It would be natural to ask about how the case was going so there would be plenty to talk about.

A sudden thought struck her. If he wasn't at breakfast, then the likelihood of seeing him before they left the hotel this morning was remote. The party would not be returning to the hotel again which meant that there was a good chance she would not see him at all before they caught the night ferry back to Liverpool. She suddenly felt very cold. Worse than that, it was more than possible that their paths would never cross again.

'Good morning Fiona. May we join you?'

She looked up to see Joan Fletcher smiling at her.

'By all means do. Although I've already eaten so I shall be leaving in a minute or two. Did you both sleep well?'

'Eventually,' Joan confessed. 'We were talking about what

happened until quite late. Do you know how Douglas and Stephanie are this morning?'

'Not yet. But I will let everyone know when I do.'

It was a good ten minutes before she could get away. 'You won't forget we are all meeting in the lounge at eight-thirty, will you? Inspector Flannery and his team need to talk to everyone.'

'I don't see why.' Greg pulled a face. 'Most of us were nowhere near where those terrorists were shooting people. We didn't even hear the gunfire.'

'I think the police want to make more enquiries about Chester Porter.'

'They've already done that,' protested Greg. 'They came and asked questions the day he disappeared.'

'Perhaps they have more evidence. I really don't know.' Fiona pushed back her chair. 'If you'll excuse me, there are several things I need to do before the meeting.'

'Before you go, Fiona. I was just wondering, I'm not sure I should bother the police about it, it might not be relevant, but...' Fiona gave her an encouraging smile and Joan continued, 'I did see something a bit odd earlier that morning before Chester disappeared.'

'I'm sure they would like to hear everything that might have a bearing on the case. I would let them decide if it's relevant at all.'

'It was as we were coming out of the university. Chester was one of the first out and this strange woman came up and thrust a brown envelope into his hands. I think Chester was a bit surprised because he stopped suddenly just looking at it then he called out after the woman, but she'd already disappeared into the crowd.'

'What did Chester do then?'

'He just stood there. To be honest, I didn't realise that it was Chester at first. Coming out from inside into the blinding light of the sun, I couldn't see so well, and I thought it was Douglas.'

'They were both wearing similar clothes that morning, I

remember. I got the two of them confused when we were waiting by the palm house,' Fiona said. 'Do you know what Chester did with the package?'

'To be honest, I wasn't paying a great deal of attention,' Joan admitted.

'I saw Stephanie talking to him,' said Greg. 'I'm not sure, but I think she took it. You can ask her when she gets back.'

Fiona's stomach gave a violent lurch, but she managed a smile. 'You may be right, and it may not be important, but I definitely think you should tell the police about it. And any other details you remember. Now I really must be going.'

It was a surprise that his mobile hadn't gone straight to voicemail.

'Peter, I'm glad I caught you. I appreciate you must be up to your eyes, but there's a couple of things I thought you might want to know straightaway. I've just had a call from David Rushworth, he's been checking the emergency contact numbers for Stephanie and Douglas. Neither of them appear to be valid numbers.'

'I see.'

'And there's something else. It might not be important but…' She repeated what Joan and Greg had just told her about the incident outside the university.

'That is very useful. Thank you, Fiona.'

Fiona let out a long sigh. At least he hadn't seemed annoyed with her for wasting his time.

When Inspector Flannery walked in through the main doors of the hotel, he was accompanied by three other plainclothes officers.

Fiona smiled and walked over. At least the interviews would be over long before they all needed to leave. It was then that she noticed the two men at the back were carrying large black bags.

'Inspector Flannery, everyone is waiting for you in the lounge.'

He gave her a cursory smile then said, 'If you'll give me a moment, Mrs Mason, I need to speak to reception first. I'll be with you directly.'

She watched as all four men walked over to the desk. A considerable amount of discussion went on. The receptionist disappeared into a back room and returned a minute or so later with Rory. After more discussion, she noticed the receptionist programming what she presumed to be room keys and handed them to the two men with bags who promptly turned and walked over to the lifts.

As the Inspector made his way back to Fiona with the other officer in his wake, she saw Rory still standing behind the desk. When he caught her eye, he gave her a smile and the thumbs up sign. She tried to hide her grin and turned to face the Inspector.

'Sorry to keep you waiting, Mrs Mason. We don't wish to keep you and the remainder of your party any longer than is necessary, so if you'd like to inform your passengers that my officer here will take statements from them one at a time. The hotel manager has allowed us to use a room alongside reception over there. We might as well speak to them in alphabetical order.'

'Would you like me to go and ask David Cox to join you?'

'That would be most kind. And then would you be good enough to return as I also need to take a written statement from you about the events that I believe you witnessed yesterday.'

'Certainly, Inspector.'

Rory was still hanging around in the reception area as she walked through the lobby. He came over to speak to her.

'Don't let that man bully you.'

'You need have no fear of that, Rory. I assure you. With all that kit, I assume those two men who went upstairs to Douglas and Stephanie's rooms were crime scene investigators, do you think?' She was pushing her luck, but she couldn't exactly ask him outright where they'd been heading.

He looked puzzled. 'I suppose so, but neither room could have been a crime scene, can they?'

'No,' she admitted. 'But both of them were badly injured yesterday. I expect they're looking for anything that might help.'

Douglas Redhill turned his head and visibly shrank back into his pillow when he saw the uniformed police officer walk into the room accompanied by a tall, grey-haired man in a charcoal three-piece suit.

'I trust you are feeling better, Mr Redhill. It must have been a very traumatic experience.' The grey-haired man smiled sympathetically. He stood at the foot of the bed and lifted the blue folder from its container and began flicking through the patient medical records.

'It was.'

'I appreciate that it is the last thing you feel like doing right now, but as I am sure you appreciate, this officer does need to take a statement from you about the events that took place.'

'I don't remember much.'

The policeman sat down in the chair by the head of the bed and took out a small notebook.

'Shall we begin with what you were doing just before you went into the clearing by the water?' the policeman asked, encouragingly.

Douglas kept his answers short and it was a long laborious business getting the man to go through his story.

The policeman looked up from his notes. 'Just to confirm, you followed one of the trails and when you arrived at the waterside you decided to sit down for a breather and the first thing you noticed was the sound of gunfire?'

Douglas nodded.

'But you didn't see the men appear out from behind the trees?'

'No.'

'Did you see anyone else that you knew by the water?'

'Don't remember?'

'Miss Jessen for example?'

Douglas stared at the policeman. 'Oh yeah. She may have been there.'

'Did you see her get shot?'

'I was too busy running.'

'I see.'

The officer scribbled into his notebook.

'Is she okay?' Douglas asked.

'I'm sorry to have to tell you that Miss Jessen died from her injuries.'

'Sorry about that,' Douglas muttered.

'Who told you and Sally to go to that particular spot, Mr Redhill?' asked the tall man suddenly.

Douglas turned his head sharply and watched as the man lifted a chair from against the wall and brought it alongside the bed opposite the policeman.

'Well, Mr Redhill?'

'No one.' Suddenly, realising his mistake he muttered, 'I don't know a Sally.'

'Come now, Mr Redhill. This is not the time to start playing games. Let us return to the man who deliberately lured you there with, as I am sure you must have worked out by now, the express intention of shooting you both. Do you honestly believe he will stop there?'

The man in the bed, blinked rapidly. 'Who are you? You're not a doctor.'

'No, Mr Redhill, or should I say, Mr Masterson, I am not. However, I am here to help you. And believe me, you are going to need our protection. Let us get straight to the point. We know who you both are, and why the pair of you came to Belfast. We are also aware that in order to achieve your objective, you had to have help. Presumably from the same person who gave you those instructions to go to the lakeside. May I remind you, Mr Masterson, that that man is a terrorist? He will stop at nothing. He has already prevented your brother's girlfriend from identifying him.

How do you think he is going to react when he hears that you are still alive?'

Edward Masterson's shoulders slumped.

'If you value your life, Mr Masterson, I suggest you tell us the whole story. Shall we start with how and when the two of you first made contact?'

Thirty

'Can you tell me what time you arrived at the Temple of the Winds, Mrs Mason?'

'Not precisely, but I would estimate that it was some time around four o'clock.'

'And you climbed to the top?' She nodded. 'What exactly could you see from there?'

The questions seemed to go on and on. How many people were in the clearing? Could she identify any of them clearly at that distance? What were Douglas Redhill and Stephanie Jessen doing exactly when she first saw them?

Inspector Flannery barely lifted his eyes from the sheet of paper as he wrote her answers firing one question after another until she had been through every detail of what happened right up to when the paramedic took Stephanie's dead body from her arms. Only then did he lower his pen and look at her directly. He still didn't seem content and insisted on going over the details a second time.

There was no point in getting annoyed. She'd brought it on herself. Her outburst at their first meeting had been totally uncalled for. Way over the top. He'd only been doing his job and she had torn into him like some demented fury. Was it any wonder she'd put the man's back up? She was in no position to object to his manner now.

'And you say once Douglas Redhill lay motionless on the ground, the gunman turned his attention to Stephanie Jessen and took aim and fired?'

'The bullet caught her just here.' Fiona put her right hand

on her upper chest spreading her fingers over her heart. 'Then she threw her arms up in the air and toppled sideways.'

'Are you sure that's what you actually saw, or do you think that is what happened? You see, I do have a problem with that, Mrs Mason. If Mr Redhill was on his feet and had covered thirty to forty yards before he fell, how come Miss Jessen still sat there all that time?'

'I remember thinking the same thing. I screamed at her to move though I was much too far away for her to hear.' She felt her heart beat faster at the memory. Taking a deep breath to steady herself, she continued, 'I can only assume, Inspector, she was paralysed with shock when the shooting began. Douglas had hold of her arm trying to pull her up when he was shot in the shoulder. That was when he turned and ran. When I looked back at Stephanie, she had pushed herself onto her knees, but she still wasn't on her feet.'

Inspector Flannery did not look convinced. The questions continued until she'd been through every detail of the gunmen's movements until they ran to the dinghy and it sped away out of sight.

The Inspector sat back and scratched his head. 'So, Mrs Mason, this gunman specifically chose Douglas Redhill and Stephanie Jessen as targets?'

'That is what it looked like to me. He didn't fire at anyone else. Just those two.'

'Perhaps he didn't have time.'

'True. But why didn't he go for easier targets? There were several people who were much closer to him. And why continue shooting at Douglas as he tried to get away? He had almost reached the edge of the clearing before he fell.'

He shook his head. 'Why would the gunman deliberately pick out two strangers who had only been in the country for less than a week?'

'Obviously, I cannot answer that, Inspector. Perhaps they were not strangers. I have no idea. I'm not a detective.'

'Exactly, Mrs Mason. You are not.'

'But, Inspector,' she said firmly, 'I do know what I saw. If you choose not to believe me, Inspector, so be it.'

They stared at each other for several minutes. Finally, it was the Inspector who dropped his gaze and looked down at the piece of paper in front of him. When he had finished checking that he had missed nothing, he pushed the form across the desk. 'I'd like you to read your statement, Mrs Mason, and if you are happy that it is a true account of what you have just told me, I would like you to sign and date it.'

She was still reading it through when there was a tap on the door and one of the CSI men who'd arrived with the Inspector came in and whispered something into his superior's ear.

The Inspector nodded and smiled to himself.

When the man had gone, she couldn't resist asking, 'I take it your officer has discovered the scarf in Stephanie's room, Inspector. Was I right? Was it a nail-file?'

The Inspector glared at her, snatched up the statement Fiona had just signed and got to his feet. With a curt 'Thank you,' he turned on his heel and marched to the door.

She shouldn't have rubbed it in. That had been petty. But she couldn't stop herself sitting back, a satisfied smile on her lips.

Edward Masterson stared at the tall grey-haired man standing by the wall who was taking the phone call. The man's face was totally impassive, but somehow, he knew that whatever information the man was now receiving did not bode well for his own future. Not that things could get much worse. Not now that he'd admitted being complicit in the death of Eamon McCollum, even if it had been Sally who'd done the actual shooting, he had driven the bike.

The phone call ended. The grey-haired man came back to the bedside and sat down in the chair once more.

'My apologies for the interruption. So, Mr Masterson, let us recap what you have told us about the man who helped you to set up this plan to avenge your brother's death. You claim he was a stranger. You know nothing about him and all you can tell us is that he had an Irish accent?'

'I told you. We never ever met him in person. Everything was done over the phone.'

'I appreciate that the initial contact was made through a Miss Nuala McBride, but I must confess that I find it somewhat difficult to believe that you would trust a total stranger, albeit that Miss McBride is a distant cousin of Sally Brent.'

A vein began to throb in his left temple. His mouth was dry. 'Sally and Nuala spent a lot of time together as kids. The families went on holiday together.'

'That may be so, but people grow up, allegiances change. Did it not occur to you that you could be being set up so that charges for attempted murder could be made against you back in England?'

'Of course, it did! I'm not stupid. But Sally was adamant that Nuala would never betray her. According to Nuala, there were a quite a few people who had Eamon McCollum at the top of their hit list. He'd made enemies of several republican sympathisers let alone the loyalist groups he'd attacked in the past. This friend of Nuala's claimed to have as great a motive as we had for getting rid of him.'

'Did he tell you what that motive was?'

'No. At least not to me, but it was Sally who did all the negotiating. Sally was even more suspicious than I was at first, and I've no idea what Nuala told her, but she managed to convince her. When I said it was all too dangerous, all Sally would say was that trust worked both ways. As far as this chap was concerned, we could be working for the security services to flush out men like him. I still wanted nothing to do with either of them, but Sally said we should consider his offer because there was no other way we would ever get close enough to McCollum. That still didn't sound convincing to me, but Sally was adamant. Said if I didn't help, she'd do it alone. The idea was the chap would tell us McCollum's routines and then it was up to us when and where we decided to take him out. Sally said, as long as the man didn't know the details of what we were planning, he couldn't betray us.'

The grey-haired man stared at him for what seemed an age, then shook his head. 'I find it hard to believe that you and Sally would make no effort to discover a great deal more about this mystery man.'

'We did. Sally may have been obsessed, but she was no fool. She used to have long girlie chats with Nuala about boyfriends and the like. Sally was convinced that our contact was her latest, and that he had to be pretty close to McCollum to know his movements.'

'But, despite your reservations, you agreed to go along with the idea?'

He gave a long sigh and nodded. 'We thought the whole plan would fall through once McCollum was arrested, but our contact said to come over to Belfast just as we'd planned anyway, and he'd arrange things for us. I wasn't happy, but to make sure that Nuala wouldn't betray us, Sally managed to trick her cousin into sending us an email. As we had no idea who this chap was, it doesn't help incriminate him as such, but it ties Nuala to the plan so we thought that would be enough.'

'Did Nuala know how you were getting to Belfast and where you would be staying?'

'No. This holiday tour was Sally's idea. She thought it was the best way to ensure that neither Nuala nor her friend would know exactly where we were. That way, neither she nor her boyfriend could give us away.'

'But he did betray you, did he not? Perhaps not by revealing what you intended to do to the authorities, but by asking you to meet him at the lakeside below the Temple of the Winds at four o'clock.'

He buried his face in his hands.

'How did you communicate with this man?'

'Through Nuala. Nuala would phone Sally on this special pay-as-you-go mobile Sally bought.'

'Did Sally have Nuala McBride's number?'

'Nuala always phoned Sally.' His brain hurt with the effort of trying to remember. 'I really don't know.'

'And it was this contact who arranged for you to pick up the gun and the bike and told you when to be ready to ride past the hospital.'

'We were waiting in the side street and when the call came that McCollum was about to leave, I started up the bike. But I've already told you all this.' Sweat beaded his forehead. He wiped it away with the back of his hand.

'True, Mr Masterson, but would you tell me once more exactly how you were given the gun and the bike.'

'I was given an envelope with the keys to a lockup and instructions where to find it.'

'And the keys to the bike were also in the envelope?'

'Yes.'

'When did you receive the envelope?'

'It was handed over as I came out of Queens University the day before.'

'But not to you personally.'

'Sorry?'

'The envelope was given to the wrong person, was it not? To Chester Porter in fact. I understand that the two of you could easily be mistaken for each other.'

The blood drained from his cheeks. 'How did you know that?'

'I know a great deal, Mr Masterson.' The penetrating stare was enough to send unpleasant sensations to his bladder. 'Is that why Chester Porter had to die?'

'His death was nothing to do with me!' His voice rose a whole octave. 'That was Sally. She saw what happened and took it from him before he had a chance to even open it. I said it didn't matter. Chester would never realise what was inside. He'd never associate it with McCollum's death, but Sally wasn't happy. She said we couldn't afford for there to be anything that might lead to us. I knew nothing about it until he went missing. You've got to believe me.'

'Did she tell you how she killed him?'

Tears began coursing down his cheeks. 'I didn't ask. I didn't want to know. The woman was mad. Ever since we arrived in Belfast, she's got more and more obsessed. I couldn't reason with her.'

Loud, high-pitched sobs echoed around the room.

Thirty-One

Fiona need not have worried that Inspector Flannery and his men would draw out the interviews and so delay the group's departure for their tour to Castle Ward. She had pointed out that they were running to a tight schedule and would need to leave promptly at eleven o'clock to be on time for their first booked activity, but she wouldn't have put it past him to deliberately hold things up.

Quite what she had done to get on the wrong side of the Inspector she wasn't sure. Perhaps he resented her input. She had to admit, it hadn't been diplomatic to make those final comments about what had been found during the search of Stephanie's room, but the way he'd tried to confuse her during the interview, suggesting she'd overhyped what she'd seen, had annoyed her.

When she saw Norman Mullins, who was the last person to be interviewed, come out of the room, Fiona decided to go down to the entrance lobby. It was a good ten minutes later before she saw the police car arrive to take the men back to the station. She got up from her seat and started to cross the lobby so that as the lift doors opened and the Inspector emerged, their paths would appear to cross without any appearance of premeditation on her part.

'Oh, Inspector, I was wondering if you had any idea how Douglas Redhill is recovering after his operation. My passengers will be most anxious to know. I did try ringing the hospital earlier, but as I am not a relative, they had no authority to pass on any information.'

He glared at her for a moment or two and she suspected that the only reason he did not ignore her altogether was because of the other officers accompanying him.

'The last I heard was that the operation went well, and he is now conscious and expected to make a full recovery.'

'That is good news. Has there been any mention of when he is likely to be discharged?'

'He'll remain in hospital for a few days, but doctors hope he'll be fit to leave in the not too distant future.'

'Thank you so much, Inspector. Everyone will be pleased to hear that.'

By the time Montgomery-Jones returned to the station, things were well underway.

Chief Superintendent Dailey sat back in his chair and looked up. 'Good work at the hospital. I thought you might be able to get some useful information, but that was a great deal more than we could have hoped for.'

'I simply caught him at the right time.' Montgomery-Jones sank onto the hard chair in front of the chief superintendent's desk.

'At least now there can be little doubt that the other deaths at the loughside were merely collateral damage, a way of covering up the deaths of those two in what would be assumed to be an attack on tourists.'

'I take it you have found Nuala McBride's number in Sally Brent's mobile phone?'

'We found a Nuala, yes. Though she avoided using surnames,' Dailey replied. 'Without the information you managed to get from Masterson, it might have taken some time for us to identify McBride.'

'Is she known to you?'

'Oh yes!' The chief superintendent gave a self-satisfied grin. 'She has what might be described as an on-off relationship with John O'Connor, which confirms our suspicions that he is Masterson's mystery man. She idolises him by all accounts and follows him around like a puppy.

He throws her a few crumbs when it suits him. He is a pretty charismatic character as far as the ladies are concerned. We've sent someone round to pick her up. Unobtrusively of course. We don't want O'Connor to get wind of it straight away. He could disappear before we can positively nail him to yesterday's shootings. We still haven't traced the inflatable, but my guess is that they put it in the back of a van and drove straight back to Belfast. That would be the easiest option. O'Connor and his men would want to establish alibis and the longer they were away, the more difficult that would be.'

'I wonder if it might be a good idea for me to have another discreet word with Salmon's informant before you question her. Presumably, he must know more about Nuala McBride even if he was unaware of the planned attack on Edward Masterson and Sally Brent.'

'Good idea.'

'Have you made any progress on the leak at the hospital? O'Connor had to have had a mole on the staff to pass on the message that Eamon McCollum was about to leave. Either that or it was one of the prison guards who accompanied him.'

Chief Superintendent Dailey shook his head. 'We do know that neither of the two guards made a call so it's relatively safe to conclude it was one of the hospital staff as you said, but we haven't made much progress there I'm afraid. We've checked all the staff records and there were no new staff in the last few months either nursing, clerical or cleaning. McCollum's intended visit was kept on a need-to-know basis only. Even his mother wasn't told and was unaware until her son walked into the room. That area of the hospital was closed off to other visitors and there were only essential staff allowed on the wing throughout the period. What you have to appreciate is that feelings run high in Belfast. People have long memories. I doubt it would be that difficult to find someone who could be persuaded if a good enough story was spun. We don't really have much idea of what we're looking for. It could be a loyalist or a republican or someone with a personal gripe against McCollum, and there are plenty of those around. It all depends on what fiction O'Connor thought might serve his purpose.'

'That is a pity. You may have difficulty pinning anything on O'Connor, especially as he seems to have used Nuala McBride as a go-between. Even if McBride was aware of what O'Connor was planning against her cousin and Masterson, it may not be easy to persuade her to give up the man if she is as infatuated with him as you suggest.'

'True. However, on a positive note, thanks to the tip off from the tour manager, we have found the nail file and scarf stashed away in Sally Brent's room. Pretty astute thinking on the part of your lady friend.'

A pained look crossed Montgomery-Jones's face. 'Mrs Mason is hardly that! She and I have worked on several cases in the past that is all.'

'If you say so. I just thought that because you took her back to the hotel after the incident at the Mount Stewart estate…'

'That was because I judged that as a witness, she had information that would prove vital evidence in the case. At that point, she was in a state of considerable shock and in no condition to be questioned. My presence was not needed at the scene and so I made the decision to stay with her. I believed the sooner I could obtain some sort of statement from her the better. And, as I am sure you will concede, that proved to be the case.'

If Chief Superintendent Dailey was taken aback at the force of Montgomery-Jones protestations, apart from a fractional raise of his eyebrows, he was diplomatic enough not to question it. 'I see.'

Montgomery-Jones rapidly regained his composure. 'As you say, she can be quite astute. She has what I would call a dogged persistence. Once she has an idea, she will gnaw at it like a bone until she reaches the marrow.'

'Not one to be easily fobbed off then?'

Montgomery-Jones looked grim. 'Annoyingly so at times.'

The chief superintendent stifled a chuckle and changed the subject. 'So, everything is beginning to fall into place.'

Montgomery-Jones rose to his feet. 'I will arrange a meeting with Salmon's informant.' He took the hunter watch from his waistcoat pocket and checked the time. 'With luck, I may be able to get him on a lunch break.'

Fiona was not in the mood to join the rest of the party wandering around the formal gardens in the half an hour or so after lunch. Instead, she went in search of Winston. There had been no time to talk to him after the morning interviews before their departure. It was too early for him to be at the coach, but he wasn't far away, sitting on a grassy slope looking down towards the lake enjoying the afternoon sun.

'Hello, sweetheart? How goes it? Come and tell me what's wrong.' He patted the patch of grass next to him and she sank down beside him. Even sitting side by side, she felt dwarfed by the bear-like West Indian.

She pulled a face. 'Nothing's wrong. I'm a bit tired that's all. I confess I won't be sad to get back home to my own bed. It may have been a relatively short tour, but it has been somewhat eventful, shall we say.' She gave him a weak smile.

He turned his head and looked directly at her. 'You can't kid me, sweetheart. Something's up. You were fine at breakfast so what's happened since? That Inspector chap upset you?'

She shook her head and let out a long sigh. 'He did give me a bit of a grilling. I'm definitely not his favourite person. He tried to make out I was making everything up just to get attention.'

'He don't know you, that's all. But you ain't one to let people like that get you down, so what is it?'

'There's no fobbing you off is there, Mr Taylor? It's just that I feel so angry.'

'With him?'

'No. With myself, I suppose. Coming over here in the coach this morning, I had time to think through everything that's happened. I'm not explaining this very well, but yesterday when Stephanie died, I was upset. She was in my care and stupid though it sounds, I felt responsible somehow. It affected me very badly. I don't really remember much after she died until I was back in my room. That hour or so is a complete blank. But then later...' She looked up at Winston who wrapped an arm around her shoulder. 'I probably should not be telling you this, but well, I found out that it was Stephanie who killed Chester.'

'So why is you angry with you's self?'

'For letting myself get so upset about Stephanie when she didn't deserve it, I suppose. I know that doesn't really make sense, but I can't help that's how I feel.'

Winston gave her a hug pulling her close. It was typical of Winston that he didn't pester her with questions. He was just there when she needed him.

'Thank you, Winston. I feel a lot better just telling you about it.' She sat up, hugging her knees to her chest.

'That's what I'm here for, sweetheart. Your job is to look after the passengers and my job is to look after you. Now that's what I like to see! You look so pretty when you's laughing.'

She gave him a mock punch. 'Flatterer!'

They sat in companionable silence for several minutes watching a couple of magpies strutting about on the slopes below and listening to their harsh rattling chatter.

Eventually, Winston asked, 'So, how went this morning's archery session? You gonna add fighting skills to your CV now?'

'I wish! Actually, I did have a go. I wouldn't normally as a tour manager, but with so few of my party left, they almost had more instructors than students, so they asked me to join in. I was useless. Absolute rubbish. I missed the target more times than I hit it, but we did have one star pupil and you'll never guess who.'

'Not the old lady?'

Fiona laughed. 'She wouldn't thank you for calling her that. But yes. It was Irene Mullins. She hit the bull's-eye nearly every shot.'

'Good for her.'

'They all seemed to enjoy it and the presentation on filming techniques, so that was great relief.' She glanced at her watch. 'I suppose they'll start drifting back in five minutes or so. Time to make a move.'

She swung her legs round to get to her knees only to discover that Winston was already on his feet holding out a hand to help pull her up. It never ceased to amaze her how such a big man who had to weigh eighteen stones, could be so nimble on his feet.

Thirty-Two

Montgomery-Jones was already sitting in one of the small booths when the informant came into the pub.

'What can I get you?' Montgomery-Jones asked as the man slid along the bench seat opposite.

'Just a half. I've got a job this afternoon.'

'Anything to eat?'

The man shook his head.

Once Montgomery-Jones returned from the bar with the two glasses and had resumed his seat, he said, 'Thank you for coming, let us get down to business. What can you tell me about Nuala McBride?'

'Nuala?' Whatever the man had been expecting it wasn't that. 'What do you want to know about her for?'

'For a start, has she been with the group long?'

'Not really.' He thought for a while. 'About eighteen months, a couple of years perhaps. John O'Connor brought her along. She works for one of the transport companies and was able to pass on useful info about certain freight coming in.'

'Is she O'Connor's girlfriend?'

'Sort of.'

'What does that mean?'

'O'Connor's not exactly a one-woman type. She throws a hissy fit now and again when he messes her about, but she keeps coming back for more. The two of them have been thick as thieves for the last couple of weeks, but something happened yesterday, and they had a real bust up.'

'Do you know what it was about?'

The man shrugged his shoulders. 'Nope. He'd been seeing another woman, I should imagine.'

'Could it have been anything to do with the attack on tourists over at Mount Stewart House?'

'You think O'Connor and his men were responsible?'

'You are a member of the CIRA. You tell me.'

There was a long silence. 'All I know is that one of the lockups we use was told to expect a delivery. I was told to be there to open it up and check that the coast was clear when the van arrived. Once I'd closed the doors, I got back in my taxi and went back to the centre.'

'Have you any idea what was inside the van?'

'Not a clue. As I said, I didn't go inside.'

'What time was this?'

'I was told to be ready for five o'clock. It didn't turn up until about ten past.'

'Can you describe the van? Did you get the number plate?'

Ten minutes later, Montgomery-Jones made a phone call.

'Great stuff!' The Chief Superintendent's voice was jubilant. 'There is no guarantee the van will still be there of course, but I'll send someone to the lockup straight away. Odds on, they were using false number plates, but we'll check anyway. And now we know exactly what we're looking for, I'll have the team go through all the CCTV cameras on the most likely roads back to the city. Plain white vans with no markings on the side are plentiful enough, but the number plate, even if it's false, should identify it. Are you coming back here?'

'I will be there as soon as I can, but I thought it best to let you know straight away.'

'Absolutely. We might even have some other news to give you by the time you get here.'

The reassurance of talking things over with Winston didn't

last. How could she have been so wrong about Stephanie? All that anguish she'd been through as she'd cradled the woman's body. It was pointless to waste her energy mulling over her own gullibility. Best to push it all to the back of her mind.

She tried to concentrate on what the guide was saying as they all trooped into the courtyard.

'For the *Game of Thrones*, these castle towers were transformed into Winterfell, where the head of House Stark rules over his people.'

It didn't help that she had never watched the popular television series so the names of the characters and the events the enthusiastic guide kept referring to, meant nothing to Fiona.

'The filming started with a pilot episode in 2009, some of which was located here at Castle Ward. If you are fans of the show, this is a very recognisable location. It is where King Robert Baratheon first arrived at Winterfell. It has also been used in many other scenes featuring the Stark family.'

Although Fiona had never seen the series, it was evident that not only Irene and Norman Mullins and Beryl and David Cox, were ardent followers of the programme. It only went to prove; one should never make assumptions about people. As she, above anyone else, should know, she thought bitterly.

'It took eight weeks to build the set of Winterfell, and then the actual filming took only four days. However, it was successfully adapted for television with filming continuing throughout 2010.'

Once the guide had finished his patter, and everyone started bombarding him with questions, Fiona could take a step back and return to her own thoughts. If only she'd had a chance to talk with Peter again before returning home. He must have some idea as to why Stephanie had felt it was necessary to kill Chester. There hadn't been any arguments between the two of them before that day as far as she knew. No antipathy. So, what had happened? Had he done something? Said something? But what could possibly be so bad that would result in her killing a virtual stranger? It didn't make any sense. Could it possibly be something to do with the envelope he'd been given that Joan Fletcher had talked about? If Stephanie took it from him, as Greg had suggested, then if nothing else, it tied the two of them together.

That wasn't the only mystery. When she'd told Inspector Flannery that the gunman had deliberately shot at Stephanie and Douglas, he'd asked what possible reason could the man have for picking on those two. Perhaps he had a point. Nonetheless, the Inspector would never convince her that they were simply chance targets out of a sizeable group of people at the scene.

Could Chester's and Stephanie's deaths and the attempt on Douglas's life be connected? Surely, they had to be.

Fiona had the feeling that both deaths had to be linked somehow to Peter's investigation. Although he had shown great interest in helping her when he'd first come over to Belfast, the death of a tourist certainly didn't warrant a senior Secret Services officer travelling all this way.

There was a definite air of optimism in the incident room at the station. Several of the men were sitting perched on desks, with mugs of coffee in their hands, laughing and talking. The only ones who still appeared to be hard at it were a team searching through CCTV footage. One of the officers pushed himself to his feet and came over to speak to Montgomery-Jones when he walked into the room.

'The chief super's in the observation room, sir.'

'Thank you. Are you all celebrating something?'

The young sergeant gave a guilty laugh. 'Sort of, sir. Looks like the case is about to be wrapped up.'

'Oh?'

'I'm sure the Chief would prefer to tell you himself, sir. Do you know where you're going, or would you like me to show you?'

'I am sure I shall be able to find it. I have no wish to pull you away from your festivities.' His smile negated any hint of criticism implied by his words.

Chief Superintendent Dailey turned away from the one-way mirror into the interview room as Montgomery-Jones pushed open the door.

'Come in, man. You should listen to this. Our Miss McBride is only too happy to tell us exactly what's been going on.'

'I heard that you had had a breakthrough.'

The chief superintendent gave a broad grin. 'I was about to send two of my detectives to bring her in when a call came through from uniform section to say officers had been called out to a violent domestic. It seems our Nuala had driven round to John O'Connor's house screaming blue murder. When he refused to let her in, she started throwing stones and breaking windows, which is when the neighbours phoned for the police. By the time they got there, she'd had a go at his precious car, which brought him out of the house to stop her. At which point, she flew at him like some demented animal and the two of them were rolling about on the lawn. The officers had a job separating them both and it ended up with them both arrested and brought in for questioning.' The chief superintendent gave a low chuckle. 'If nothing else, we can charge O'Connor with attacking a police officer. One of the PC's ended up with a right shiner.'

The interview was evidently well underway as Montgomery-Jones took a seat alongside Dailey to observe what was happening. He had a clear view of a very animated Nuala McBride sitting across the table from the two officers.

'Should you be interviewing her without her lawyer being present?' Montgomery-Jones asked.

'She has been asked if she wants one and offered the duty solicitor but refused. It's all on the tape. According to her, all he will do is tell her to make no comment and to use her words, she has "every intention of letting the police know exactly what that bastard has done," and no one is going to stop her even if that means she has to spend the next ten years in gaol for unintentionally aiding and abetting.'

'So, let me just clarify, Miss McBride, you phoned Sally Brent to tell her and Edward Masterson to be at the loughside in the clearing below the Temple of the Winds at four o'clock, but you had no idea that O'Connor and his men intended to shoot them both?'

'Of course not! She was my cousin, for God's sake. We grew up together.'

'Why did you think O'Connor wanted them to be there?

'The original deal was that John would set up the two of them with all they needed to shoot Eamon McCollum – the bike, the guns and so on, and make sure the two of them got away hiding all the stuff in a van in a side street in exchange for two thousand quid. John told me that this meeting yesterday was for them to hand over the cash.'

'It was a long way to go. Why not do the handover in Belfast?'

'John wanted them to come to the warehouse, but Sally refused. Said it had to be in public. The police were snooping around the group because of what happened to one of the passengers, the one that was mugged. She was the one who suggested Mount Stewart House. She obviously didn't trust him, and she was right, wasn't she?' Her fists banged on the table.

'But why would O'Connor kill them both? He wouldn't even get the money.'

'I don't know, do I? Ask John!' Nuala folded her arms and sat back in the chair, a defiant look on her face.

The DCI looked down at the notes he'd made.

'I wonder,' said Montgomery-Jones softly as though talking to himself.

'What is it?' asked Chief Superintendent Dailey.

'Ask if the two women ever talked about their boyfriends.'

The Chief Superintendent switched on the

communication link and passed on the request.

The DCI dropped the pen he was holding back on the table and sat back looking across at Nuala.

'How well did you know Sally? You say you grew up together, but what about lately? Had you spoken much before O'Connor asked you to make contact?'

'I suppose we'd lost touch these last few years,' she admitted.

'Did you chat much about the old times or was it all about the job?'

'Mostly about the job, but we talked a bit about Philip, Edward's brother. She said she still thought about him every day. She hadn't been out with anyone else since.'

'What about your boyfriends. Did you tell her about them?'

'She asked and I told her there was someone special.' Nuala seemed reticent to say much more.

'So, you told her about John?'

'A bit, but not that he was the one who was arranging for the pair of them to take out McCollum,' she added hastily.

'Do you know if Sally had been in touch with any of your family?'

There was a long silence before Nuala said, 'Danuta mentioned she'd had a call just to say she was thinking of coming over to Belfast and perhaps we could all meet up for a coffee or something.'

'Who is Danuta?'

'My sister. But it was just the one call. I didn't even know they'd been in touch until a few days ago.'

Montgomery-Jones sat back, a satisfied smile on his face.

'You think Sally put two and two together?' asked Dailey.

'Edward Masterson said she was very shrewd. I would think Sally discovered all there was to know about Nuala's boyfriend from her sister.'

'So that when O'Connor discovered Sally knew who he was, he had to make sure she could never testify against him.'

'You said he was ruthless.'

Chief Superintendent Dailey nodded. 'We haven't been able to interview O'Connor as yet. We're still waiting for his lawyer to turn up.'

'I wonder what happened to the money. Masterson did not have it on him when he arrived at the hospital. I believe I am correct in saying that all he had was found in the contents of his pockets. Do we know what happened to his rucksack?'

'There were a great many bags, coats and associated clutter left at the scene after the incident. A great deal of it couldn't be identified. I would have thought all the bags would have been searched if only to find the owners. I'll ask for them to take another look.'

'I doubt it was in loose bundles. It may well have been sealed in some kind of package and easily overlooked if no one was looking for it specifically.'

'True, true.' The Superintendent nodded. 'One thing I haven't yet told you is that the van was still in the lockup with the dinghy, guns and balaclavas still inside. And guess what else?'

Montgomery-Jones's eyes widened. 'Not the Norton?'

'Yep. One motorbike plus two sets of leathers and two black helmets. The fingerprint guys are working overtime going through the lot. The rate things are going, Andrew Salmon's informant won't be needed at any trial, so he won't be put at risk.'

'Salmon will be pleased to know that. Talking of Salmon, it is probably time I rang him to report on progress.'

Thirty-Three

The last part of the tour to Castle Ward was the photo opportunity. The idea of dressing up in any kind of fancy costume was something of an anathema to Fiona and she'd never been keen to have her photo taken at the best of times. She was surprised that even Greg and Joan Fletcher who, like her, did not possess Sky TV and so had never seen the show, were more than happy to join the others. At least, it provided Fiona with an opportunity to creep away for a quiet half hour and put herself in a better frame of mind by phoning her sons.

It would still be early morning in Canada. At home, back in Guildford, she would time her call just before lunch when she would be able to speak to her grandchildren. She might still be lucky enough to catch them at breakfast. For the last few months, Adam and Kristie had been taking the children for swimming lessons at the local pool. With luck, she might just catch them before they left.

She let the phone ring for almost a full minute and was about to cut off the call when Adam picked up.

'You sound a bit breathless.'

'Oh hi, Mum. That's because I've only just walked back in the door. Can I ring you back later? Kristie's already in the car with the kids ready to take them to the pool, but she's forgotten Adam junior's arm bands. I'll ring you back as soon as I've dropped them off.'

'No problem, darling. I appreciate I don't normally ring till much later.'

She rang off and trudged back to the costume room.

Most of her passengers had chosen long capes with fur collars, but the capes were far too long for Beryl and she was having difficulty finding something suitable. In the end, she settled for a short leather jerkin no doubt worn by one of the children in the cast.

As everyone sorted through the selection of swords and bows on offer, Fiona's mobile began to buzz.

'Hello, darling. That was quick.'

There was a slight pause before a voice said, 'Good afternoon to you too, Fiona.'

'Peter!' Even to her own ears, her voice sounded shrill. 'I'm so sorry, I thought it was Adam.'

'I rather gathered that.' He gave a low chuckle.

'Hold on a minute while I go to somewhere a little quieter.'

It was only a few seconds before she was well out of earshot of anyone else, but it did at least give her a few vital moments to let her heart return to normal and a chance to gather her thoughts. 'That's better. How is the case going?'

'Thanks to you, I believe we are almost there.'

'With your case or mine?'

He gave a low chuckle. 'Both.'

'I don't suppose you are going to tell me what's happening.'

'You know very well I am in no position to do that, at least not as the investigation stands at present. However, when everything is concluded, I would be happy to answer your questions. Without your help, we certainly could not have brought things to such a satisfactory conclusion so quickly. Thank you, Fiona.'

'No problem,' she mumbled.

'However, the reason I phoned is to ask if you would let me take you out for dinner when we both return home.'

When Fiona did not answer straight away, he said, 'If you would prefer not to, I quite understand.'

'It's not that, Peter. I would love to have dinner with you.

It's just that I appreciate that in the normal course of such things, it might be sometime before the case goes to court and, well I'm not sure my curiosity can wait for answers that long.'

He laughed. 'Patience is not one of your many virtues, is it?'

'I've never pretended it was. Seriously, Peter. You implied the information I gave you was helpful in solving the case. I feel I'm entitled to know if my suppositions were correct.'

She heard the sound of laughter behind her and turned to see David and Beryl closely followed by the others walking over towards where the coach was parked.

'I'm sorry, Peter, I have to go. Give me a buzz when you get back to London. Bye.'

'Take care of yourself.'

Fiona was not the only person Montgomery-Jones needed to call.

'Good to hear things are going so well, Peter. It looks as though the case is pretty much sewn up now.' Andrew Salmon sounded ecstatic after Montgomery-Jones had brought him up to date on everything that had been happening.

'I think there is still some way to go yet. The only answer John O'Connor would give at interview was "No comment", which is exactly what we expected. That will not prevent him from being charged and taken to court. Chief Superintendent Dailey is convinced there is enough to convict him.'

'You don't sound so sure.'

'Only in as much as I do not believe in celebrating before the event. We do have Nuala McBride's evidence, much of which can be substantiated including the money that Masterson took with him to the proposed meeting, which the team have recovered from one of the rucksacks left at the scene. It will take a little longer to identify the fingerprint evidence from the van and its contents, but the first signs look hopeful. There were no prints on any of the gun barrels – either the gunmen wore gloves or they were wiped – but the forensic team did manage to lift fingerprints from the inflatable and from the clothing that was abandoned with the rest of the kit.'

'Really? I knew that it was possible in theory, but I didn't think the process was generally available.'

'And presumably neither did the CIRA. It would seem, however, that the seriousness of the situation justifies the cost.'

'And you say Dailey doesn't think it will be necessary for my man to give evidence?'

'If matters go as he anticipates, then no. However, nothing can be guaranteed until all the evidence is in. The Chief Superintendent believes that once they hear that O'Connor and his cronies were responsible for McCollum's death, many of McCollum's old guard will testify against O'Connor.'

'That's a long shot, isn't it?'

'Who knows?'

'Anyway, when are you intending to come back to London?'

'I would like to get back as soon as possible, but I cannot see that happening for a few more days at least.'

'Best of luck, anyway. And thanks for all you've done. I appreciate it. I owe you one.'

'Indeed, you do, Andrew. Indeed, you do.

Montgomery-Jones ended the call, a smile spreading over his handsome features.

Thirty-Four

The booking made for their Irish evening had been for twelve people – her original compliment of eleven passengers plus Fiona. She tried to persuade Winston to join them, but he was reluctant to do so. Much as she would like her driver's company for his own sake, it would have been even more reassuring to have him with her. So many empty seats at the table would be a constant reminder of all that had happened and put a dampener on their tour's final celebration.

As they left Castle Ward and were driving back to Belfast, it was Irene who brought up the subject again.

'As it's our last evening all together, you are joining us this time aren't you, Winston?'

Winston smiled and shook his head.

'I've already tried to persuade him,' said Fiona.

'But why not?'

'You don't want me there,' Winston protested.

The noisy clamour from the back of the coach indicated otherwise.

'We wouldn't ask you if we didn't want you to come,' insisted Beryl.

Fiona laughed. 'I have no wish to end the tour attempting to quell a riot, so I think you'd better agree.'

'They won't like it at Head Office,' Winston protested.

'I've already spoken to David Rushworth and he agrees that as the place is already paid for, it would be a waste for you not to use it. So, that's settled.'

There were cheers all round.

The coach pulled into the small car park outside the Public House in plenty of time to let everyone freshen up before the festivities were due to begin. There were a few cars already parked.

'We won't be shown into the dining room until about ten minutes before the entertainment starts so if you'd all like to take yourselves to the bar, you can get yourself a drink while you're waiting.'

'Should we take our coats?' asked Norman.

'Winston will lock the coach so there's no need to take more than you require for the evening. When we leave here, we'll be driving straight to the ferry so you might like to sort yourselves out now as I'm not sure how much time there will before we are asked to board the ferry.'

Several passengers decided to repack their hand luggage, so everyone left the coach in dribs and drabs. Fiona waited patiently until Greg, the last passenger, followed his wife down the steps, leaving her alone with Winston.

'I'm so glad you decided to join us, Winston. I really don't think I could have enjoyed the evening knowing you were sitting out here in the coach for two hours.'

'I'm used to sitting around, sweetheart. It goes with the job. Besides, I'd have gone in the bar.'

He locked the coach and they started to stroll over to the entrance.

'I think there's someone over there waiting to have a chat with you,' Winston said, his voice barely above a whisper.

Fiona wasn't sure she'd heard him correctly. 'What? Who?'

'Over there, standing by his car.' He nodded his head to the back corner of the car park. 'I'll leave you two alone.'

She turned to see a familiar tall figure walking towards her. Her heart gave a small leap. She'd regained a little of her composure by the time Peter had caught up with her. 'This is a surprise. Are you here for the Irish evening too? There are still a couple of spare seats at our table. Would you like to join us? I know the others won't mind.' She knew she was gabbling, but she couldn't stop herself.

'Much as I would love to spend the evening with you, I need to return to the station in a short while. I came because I decided that perhaps you were correct and given all the help you gave pointing us in the right direction, that you had a right to know if your ideas proved to be correct.' He glanced around. 'However, I am not sure that standing in the middle of a car park is really the most suitable place to talk.'

'It might be a little noisy in the bar.' Plus, though she wouldn't dream of saying it, she'd prefer her passengers not to see her talking to a tall handsome stranger. Having to explain who he was might prove a little tricky.

'True. We can either sit in my car or we could see if there is a table in the beer garden where it might be a little quieter.'

'That sounds like a good idea. Shall we go and find out?'

Fiona brushed the seat of the wooden bench at one of the four battered picnic tables on a patchy square of grass and sat down. As she waited for Peter to return with the drinks, she tried to get a grip on her churning emotions by attempting to concentrate on all the questions she needed him to answer.

'Not exactly the most attractive setting,' he said placing the two glasses of lime and soda on the rickety table.

Fiona glanced around at the half-dead unpruned shrubs draped against two of the somewhat dilapidated creosoted wooden fences that bordered the beer garden

'True, but at least we'll be able to hear each other out here. So, was I right? Was Stephanie responsible for Chester's death?'

'It would appear so. And you were correct about the nail-file and the scarf.'

'But why did she kill him?'

Peter sighed. 'That I cannot tell you.'

When he saw the look on her face, he added quickly, 'At

the moment, all we have is speculation.'

'Could it be something to do with the package that Chester was given as we came out of the university?'

He nodded and took a sip of his drink. 'That would appear to be a likely explanation.'

'Then presumably, the woman who delivered it made a mistake. She should have given it to Douglas.' He nodded. 'Do you know what was in it?'

When he didn't answer, she looked across the table holding his gaze. 'But you can't tell me.'

'Something like that.'

'Which only goes to prove what I've thought all along. That somehow, Chester's death is related to the case you came over to investigate. Interesting that you arrived the day after that terrorist was shot coming out of the hospital.'

'Do not push too far, Fiona.'

'But surely you can tell me if that was why Stephanie and Douglas were killed?'

'The investigation is still ongoing.' There was a long pause before he added, 'But that is not an unreasonable assumption.'

'What about Douglas, assuming that was his real name, which I'm beginning to doubt? When he recovers, will he be charged with anything?'

'I can only repeat, the investigation is still ongoing.'

'Which I take it means yes. I must admit, I find it hard to think of him as a killer, but I'd have said exactly the same about Stephanie. That day, both he and Stephanie came with us to the Belfast Titanic after lunch, but I suppose there was nothing to stop them slipping away once everyone was left to their own devices. The hospital wasn't that far away.'

Peter's face remained inscrutable, but he didn't contradict her.

'The question is why. I've been searching through the internet.' She ran a finger around the rim of her glass before looking at him from under her lashes. 'You'd be surprised about how much there is about this Eamon McCollum character. There was quite a bit about a previous trial about the bombing of a police station. Seems the prosecution's case disintegrated when a young man died in a hit and run, and the two other witnesses suddenly withdrew their statements.'

'Really?'

'Apparently, the young man's brother accused McCollum of ordering the hit. He made a big thing of swearing he would avenge his brother's death.'

'Understandable, I suppose, but certainly not something to condone.'

'The young man had a girlfriend. Quite a vengeful lady by all accounts.'

'If you say so.' A smile played on Peter's lips.

'I can imagine a scenario where the two arrange to come over to Belfast to carry out that threat. Incognito of course.'

'Naturally.'

'A coach party would make excellent cover, don't you think.'

'I agree.'

'Even so, they would need help.'

'I expect so.'

'But thieves fall out, don't they say?'

'So I have heard.' He lifted his glass and swallowed the last of his lime and soda. 'I should be getting back.'

'Peter Montgomery-Jones. You really are the most infuriating person I have ever met.'

He laughed and put a hand over hers giving it a brief squeeze. 'I could say exactly the same about you, Mrs Mason.'

She glared at him for a moment before her shoulders relaxed and she said, 'Touché.'

'I promise when the case is finally settled, I will answer all your questions in full, but until then…' He shrugged his shoulders.

'I'll hold you to that.'

They both got to their feet. 'You have not finished your

drink.'

She looked down at her half empty glass. 'No matter.'

They walked back to the car park. When he reached his car, he turned and said, 'As soon as I know when I am coming back to London, I will give you a ring and we will fix a date for that dinner.'

'Looking forward to it.'

He bent to kiss her – a light brush of the lips. 'We need to talk about us.'

'Is there an us?'

'That is what we need to talk about.'

He kissed her again, a longer, more lingering embrace, then got into the car.

As he slowly drove towards the road, she followed. By the time he'd found a space in the traffic to pull out, Fiona was at the door of the pub. She stood watching as the car disappeared then turned and went inside.

She still had a smile on her face when she walked into the bar. Winston was sitting on a high stool and she walked over to join him.

'Your fella gone then?'

Fiona felt the colour rushing to her cheeks. 'I keep telling you he's not my fella.'

Winston gave a low chuckle.

'Sweetheart, the only people who don't seem to know that the two of you's an item, is you and him.'

ABOUT THE AUTHOR

Judith has three passions in life – writing, travel and ancient history. Her novels are the product of those passions. Her Fiona Mason Mysteries are each set on coach tours to different European countries and her history lecturer Aunt Jessica, accompanies travel tours to more exotic parts of the world.

Born and brought up in Norwich, she now lives with her husband in Wiltshire. Though she wrote her first novel (now languishing in the back of a drawer somewhere) when her two children were toddlers. There was little time for writing when she returned to work teaching Geography in a large comprehensive. It was only after retiring from her headship, that she was able to take up writing again in earnest.

Life is still busy. She spends her mornings teaching Tai Chi and yoga or at line dancing, Pilates and Zumba classes. That's when she's not at sea as a cruise lecturer giving talks on ancient history, writing and writers or running writing workshops.

***

Find out more about Judith at www.judithcranswick.co.uk

Printed in Great Britain
by Amazon